Additional Praise for THIS IS YOUR LIFE, HARRIET CHANCE!

"[*This Is Your Life, Harriet Chance!*] is infused with Evison's characteristic empathy and heart and humor. Its tension emanates from the relationships Harriet has botched and from our changing understanding of who she is and what's at risk. As a writer, [Evison's] got a talent for character, emotion and pacing."

—*Los Angeles Times*

"Slowly, and with admirable, dark precision, Evison lays Harriet bare.... With a touch of snark and a lashing of perfectly affected irony, he flenses her to the bone and, somehow, seems kind in doing it. It is Evison's timing—the slow burn and perfect pacing of the reveals—that makes *This Is Your Life, Harriet Chance!* hang together. And with Harriet Chance—poor, frustrated, flummoxed Harriet—Evison has found his ideal foil."

—NPR Books

"It's hard to imagine a family member of any family who won't see something familiar in Harriet's quest to understand her spouse, her children and herself. And when the expected but still jarring ending unfolds, it's hard to imagine the reader who won't be moved by this lively, lovely work." —*The Denver Post*

"The book's lesson is more an affirmation than revelation: Life is hard and complicated; everyone has secrets, and even that unassuming old woman you see standing quietly at the bow of the boat has endured drama and betrayal and passion. In the end, the sweetness overrides the sorrows. *This Is Your Life, Harriet Chance!* is a lively, entertaining read, funny and poignant."

—*Star Tribune* (Minneapolis)

"[An] insightful, richly entertaining look at a woman who, very late in the game, finds that life remains full of surprises.... Evison writes humanely and with good humor of his characters, who, like the rest of us, muddle through, too often without giving ourselves much of a break. A lovely, forgiving character study that's a pleasure to read."

—*Kirkus Reviews* (starred review)

"Evison's voice is buoyant and cheeky as he unveils the deep traumas that form Harriet's sense of herself.... Evison succeeds in crafting a believable and gut-wrenching story, particularly Harriet's relationship with her daughter and their efforts to accept and love one another." —*Publishers Weekly*

"Evison alternates between a cheeky narration of Harriet's past and present.... It echoes the cinematic approach of Evison's previous work, painting a vivid picture that's easy for a reader to immerse him or herself in.... A book of secrets, *This Is Your Life, Harriet Chance!* reveals how one or two choices can dramatically alter not only the course of your life, but the lives of many others." —*BookPage*

"A generous and wise tale, told with Evison's trademark verve and charisma, *This Is Your Life, Harriet Chance!* is a deeply felt and deeply comforting novel."

—Patrick deWitt, author of *The Sisters Brothers*

"Once again, Jonathan Evison dazzles. *This Is Your Life, Harriet Chance!* is as sweet as it is inventive, profound as it is hilarious, unflinching as it is big-hearted. Step right up, don't be shy! Take the hand of Evison's delightfully menacing master of ceremonies and let him lead you into the kaleidoscopic journey of your life."

—Maria Semple, author of *Where'd You Go, Bernadette*

"Jonathan Evison is a ridiculously gifted storyteller: racing, breathless, and vibrant with his prose, hungry for personal truths, and clearly in love with the world around us all. That compassion and those writerly charms are deeply felt in *This Is Your Life, Harriet Chance!*, an irresistible, inventive novel full of important ideas about how we live our lives as parents, children, partners, and human beings."

—Jami Attenberg, author of *The Middlesteins*

"*This Is Your Life, Harriet Chance!* has all the wonderful snap and sizzle we've come to expect from Jonathan Evison's work, and as much heart as any novel I've read in recent years. Jonathan packs an entire life—many lives—into this fine book, and does so with the empathy and insight of a writer at the top of his game."

—Ben Fountain, author of *Billy Lynn's Long Halftime Walk*

Also by JONATHAN EVISON

All About Lulu
West of Here
The Revised Fundamentals of Caregiving

THIS IS
YOUR LIFE,
HARRIET
CHANCE!

A Novel

JONATHAN EVISON

HARPER
PERENNIAL

Published by Harper Perennial, an imprint of HarperCollins Publishers Ltd,
by arrangement with Algonquin Books of Chapel Hill,
a division of Workman Publishing Company Inc., New York.

First published in Canada by Harper Avenue,
an imprint of HarperCollins Publishers Ltd,
in an original trade paperback edition: 2015
This Harper Perennial trade paperback edition: 2016

HarperCollins books may be purchased for educational, business, or
sales promotional use through our Special Markets Department.

HarperCollins Publishers Ltd
2 Bloor Street East, 20th Floor
Toronto, Ontario, Canada
M4W 1A8

www.harpercollins.ca

Library and Archives Canada Cataloguing in Publication
information is available upon request

ISBN 978-1-44344-294-7

Design by Anne Winslow

Printed and bound in the United States
RRD 9 8 7 6 5 4 3 2 1

FOR MOM

November 4, 1936
(HARRIET AT ZERO)

Here you come, Harriet Nathan, tiny face pinched, eyes squinting fiercely against the glare of surgical lamps, at a newly renovated Swedish hospital, high on Seattle's First Hill. It's an unseasonably chilly Wednesday in autumn, and the papers are calling for snow. Roosevelt by a landslide! they proclaim. Workers grumbling in Flint, Michigan! In Spain, a civil war rages.

Meanwhile, out in the corridor, your father paces the floor, shirtsleeves rolled to the elbow. Clutching an unlit Cuban cigar, he checks his wristwatch. He's got a three-o'clock downtown.

By the end of the week, Harriet, you'll leave the hospital wrapped in a goose-down swaddler knit by your ailing grandmother. Your father will miss his three-o'clock today. But let's not get ahead of ourselves here. They don't call it labor for nothing. Let's not forget the grit and determination of your mother. All that panting and pushing, all that clenching and straining, eyes bulging, forehead slick with sweat. Let's take a moment to appreciate the fact that she won't begrudge you any of it, though you'll always be your father's girl.

Here you come, better late than never: a face presentation. Not the boy your father so desperately wanted, but here you come, anyway, all six pounds three ounces of you. Button nose, conical head, good color. A swirl of dark hair atop your little crown. And a healthy pair of lungs, too.

Listen to you wail, as the doctor slaps your fanny: your cries, phlegmy and protracted. Hear them? These are virtually the last sounds you will utter until well after your second birthday.

Yes, Harriet, you were an exceptionally quiet child. Too quiet.

Exhibit A: December 31, 1936. For the rest of their lives, your parents will regale you, and anyone who will listen, with a rollicking story about a certain New Year's Eve party on the north end. The story involves a bassinet into which your father, in a moment of stoned clarity and admirable foresight, fastened you by your ankles and armpits for safety, using his own necktie and a leather belt from the host's closet. The party is a triumph, as the story goes, with Bacchus leading the charge. The music is brassy, the walls are thrumming. So frenzied the celebration, in fact, that amid their merrymaking, revelers fail to notice the upended bassinet in the corner. That is, until whiz kid, Charlie Fitzsimmons, the firm's youngest partner, lipstick on his collar, ladies' underpants adorning the crown of his head, nearly trips on you on his way back from the punch bowl.

It will not be the last time Charlie Fitzsimmons takes notice of you.

"Would you look at that glass of milk?" he shouts.

For an instant, the party is struck dumb as everyone turns their attention to the corner. Look at Harriman Nathan's girl!

"She'll make a hell of a judge," observes Charlie.

And of course, hilarity ensues. The story never fails, and you're the punch line, Harriet.

There you are, for God only knows how long, upside down, your poker face turning from red to blue to purple, your little gray eyes gazing impassively at the world, as your parents ring in a prosperous 1937.

You never made a peep.

This is your life, Harriet. The beginning, anyway.

August 11, 2015
(HARRIET AT SEVENTY-EIGHT)

Harriet finds Father Mullinix in his stuffy office behind the chapel, his reading glasses roosting halfway down the bridge of his nose, his laptop propped open in front of him.

He's on his feet before she can cross the threshold. "Harriet, you're shivering. Sit." He lowers her into a straight-backed chair. "My goodness, you're sopping wet."

"He's here, Father," she says. "I found his slippers this morning next to mine in the breakfast nook."

Father Mullinix smiles patiently, setting his big hands on the desktop. "We've talked about this several times recently, Harriet. There's but one ghost in the Bible, and we both know who that is."

"But last week, the WD-40. And now this."

Drawing a weary breath, Father Mullinix holds it in.

"You don't understand," says Harriet. "The WD-40, that was him, telling me to quiet those hinges on the dishwasher. He hated the squeaking."

Slowly, Father Mullinix releases his breath. Clasping his hands together on the desktop, he proceeds expertly in a measured tone.

"Perhaps it is possible he's trying to speak to you through God," he concedes. "But certainly I wouldn't take the WD-40 as a sign. Perhaps you left it there on the chair, a lapse in memory. It happens to me daily. Yesterday I found these very glasses in the pantry. We're all so busy in these times, so preoccupied. And you of all people, Harriet, you are so diligent in all things, particularly for someone of your . . . experience."

"But I know I didn't leave it there. And the slippers."

"Well, I'm sure there's an explanation."

"I saw him Father, I felt him. Last night, we were at the Continental Buffet. He was eating corned beef."

"Ah, I see. You've had another dream."

"I wasn't dreaming. He was an actual presence."

Father Mullinix smiles sadly, but Harriet can tell his patience is wearing thin. For months, she's been eating up his time, unloading her grief on him, bludgeoning him with the details of her dream life and, most recently, trying in vain to convince him that Bernard still lingered somehow in the earthly realm. Perhaps she was mistaken in confiding in him this time, though he'd never failed her in the past.

"Do you think I'm, oh, Father . . . you don't think I'm . . . ?"

"I think, perhaps, you could use some rest, Harriet."

"But Father, I assure you I'm—"

"Please, let me drive you home, Harriet."

September 9, 1957
(HARRIET AT TWENTY)

Look at you, Harriet, a grown woman! No longer a glass of milk but a tall drink of water. Okay, not so tall. Maybe a little on the squat side, maybe a little pudgy, to hear your mother tell it. But your hygiene is fastidious, your bouffant is formidable. And you're still quiet, which makes you popular among lawyers and men alike. But you've no time for men. You're a professional. Marriage is one negotiation that can wait. First, your own apartment. An automobile. A promotion.

The sky is the limit!

Here you are, at Fourth and Union, top floor, just three months removed from your associate's degree. And not your father's firm, either. Sure, you had a push, a few advantages in life, but you got here on your own. No, you'll never be a lawyer, but a crack legal assistant is not out of the question. You love your job. Okay, maybe *love* is a bit strong. But prepping documents, writing summaries, filing motions, all of it agrees with you. Look at you, downtown girl: chic but pragmatic. Shopping at Frederick & Nelson! Lunching at the Continental Buffet!

Let's be honest, though. Let's talk about the problem that has no name. All these months later, they're still slapping your fanny around the office. Your salary doesn't stretch that far. The work is exhausting. As both a woman and an assistant, you're expected to work harder. And for what? A string of pearls? A sleek automobile? A slap on the can from a junior partner? It will be six more years before Friedan exposes the "feminine mystique," twelve more before Yoko Ono proclaims woman as "the nigger of the world." But by God, Harriet Chance, you're determined to buck your disadvantages. Okay, maybe determined is a bit strong; how about resigned to them? The least you can do is achieve independence. Tackle adulthood on your own terms. Put that associate's degree to some purpose.

Make a name for yourself, Harriet Nathan.

The truth you're not telling anyone, especially not your father, is that amid the administrative whirlwind of the office, the hustle and bustle of downtown, the ceaseless tedium of legal research, you yearn for something less exhausting: for stability, predictability, and yes, a Christmas hearth festooned with stockings.

You yearn, too, Harriet, for a man. C'mon, admit it.

So, what is it about this new young building superintendent that catches your attention in the hallway upon your return from lunch, as he explains to your boss, in layman's terms even you can understand, the difference between AC and DC? Surely, it's not his stature. He's two inches shorter than you. And it turns out, he's not all that young, at thirty-three. There is, however, a squareness to his shoulders, a symmetry to his face, a quiet confidence in his bearing. Not just the firm, but the whole building—all that concrete and steel, all that electricity, all that plumbing—is reliant upon his capability. You're not alone. The whole office is impressed by his confidence, charmed by his forthrightness. Even the partners, those pompous autocrats, bulging at the waist, those experts who defer to no one, treat this man as an equal.

But here's the thing: tending an elevator, a fan, a heating duct, in his neatly creased work trousers, penlight clutched between his teeth, as he reaches for his tool belt, exposing the gray Semper Fi tattoo on his inside wrist, he strikes you as more than their equal.

Harriet Nathan, meet Bernard Chance, your valentine for 1957.

April 6, 2015
(HARRIET AT SEVENTY-EIGHT)

A phone is ringing. Slippers pad down the hallway of a large, otherwise quiet house in the flats of Carlsborg. Three bedrooms, two and one-half bathrooms, in the banana belt. With mountain views. Convenient shopping. Imagine country living in this dream home on 2.5 acres!

A spotted hand picks up the receiver and answers in a voice dry and brittle as a wheat cracker. "Hello?"

"May I please speak to Bernard Chance?"

The voice on the other end is also female, slightly stiff.

"I'm afraid he passed in November."

"I see, I'm so sorry. Is this—?"

"This is his wife, Harriet."

"Well, I guess that explains it. I'm so sorry."

"Explains what, dear? To whom am I speaking?"

"This is Janis Segress from the Ann and Virginia Nitter-house Foundation. Mr. Chance never picked up his gift basket after our silent auction last fall—wait, let's see, 2013, so, that's two falls ago. The voucher expires at the end of August."

"Voucher?"

"The Alaskan cruise? He never mentioned it?"

"Bernard? Alaska? This is the first I've heard of it. Are you certain you have the right Bernard Chance?"

"One thirty-six Rake's Glen?"

"Yes, that's us."

"We've been trying to reach him for months at 491-2318, but that number is no longer in service."

"Oh, that was his cellular telephone, dear. He never cared much for the device. He swore it would give him a brain tumor."

"I see."

"Of course, he went much quicker than he might have with a brain tumor. Physically, anyway."

"Well, that's a blessing, I'm sure."

"It was no blessing, dear, let me tell you."

"Well, I'm certainly sorry to hear it. You're welcome to—"

"Unless you consider urinating in Walmart a blessing."

"I see, well, as I was about to s—"

"Or wandering Cline Spit in your pajamas."

"Yes, well, I'm certainly glad we were able to track you down before the—"

"I was outmatched, dear. It's that simple. I was an old woman myself. Who was I to think I could care for anybody under the circumstances?"

"Mm. I see. Well," says the voice. "At any rate, our offices are located on—"

"He was still quite strong, physically, you understand. Overpowering at times. But that was only part of the problem."

"Uh-huh, yes, I see. As I was saying, our offices are located on North Sequim Avenue at West Hendrickson—kitty-corner to Jace Real Estate."

"It's a cruel process, aging. Take my advice, dear, maintain your independence as long as possible."

"I'll be sure and do that, Mrs. Chance. Now, you're welcome to redeem your gift anytime between ten a.m. and four p.m., Tuesday through Friday."

"Don't let the world push you around. Stick up for yourself, dear."

"Yes, I'll be sure and do that. And Mrs. Chance: congratulations!"

"Thank you, dear."

Replacing the phone receiver, Harriet pads back down the hallway to the foyer, where Bernard's blue windbreaker droops like a windless flag off the coatrack, a book of crosswords jutting out of the side pocket. On her way past, she stoops to straighten his sneakers.

"Hmph. Alaska," she says, straightening up. "What on earth were you thinking, dear?"

She retires to the kitchen, sets the kettle to boiling, and lays out two mugs in the breakfast nook.

"Well, you can hardly expect me to go alone," she says, unsheathing a tea bag. "It's true, I could always take Mildred. Oh, but dear, do I have to go? Would you be hurt if I didn't? You know I'm not a traveler. What you were thinking? A cruise?"

Just as the kettle is about to hiss, she hoists it off the burner and proceeds filling the mugs. "Oh, fine, then. I'll ask her. Are you happy now?"

August 15, 2015
(BERNARD, DECEASED, DAY 277)

Forgettable dress shirt, forgettable tie, pattern baldness: CTO Charmichael is nothing like Bernard expected. But then, none of this is what he expected.

"Mr. Chance, please sit down," Charmichael says, without looking up from the manila folder splayed open before him.

Chief transitional officer, you'd think he'd have a bigger desk. Something in mahogany. But no, it's institutional, bland and sturdy. A vice principal's desk. In fact, the whole office screams high school administration—the cork bulletin board, the squat gray filing cabinets, the rotary pencil sharpener.

"I presume you know why you're here?" he says, still not looking up from the file.

"Actually, no, sir."

Finally, Charmichael looks up, engaging Bernard's gray eyes meaningfully. "A little matter with some household lubricant, for starters."

"Sir?"

"Some wandering slippers? Starting to ring a bell, Candidate Chance?"

"Ah," says Bernard. "That."

Charmichael furrows his brow. "Strictly forbidden, you understand. As is eating, for the record. Yes, even in dreams."

"I thought that—"

"*Any* contact is forbidden, Candidate Chance. Regardless of the nature. This was all in the orientation, as well as the manual. Hard to miss, really. Section One, as a matter of fact. Was that not perfectly clear?"

"Uh, yessir. Yessir, it was, or I thought it was. Forgive me, sir."

"Believe me, I'm trying, we all are. There's hope for you, Chance. That's why you're here. If there wasn't hope for you, you'd be . . . well, somewhere else."

"But, sir, the thing is, she has no idea what's coming. The shock might be too much. I gotta get to her, I gotta explain."

"By my reckoning, Candidate Chance, you had nearly four decades to do that. Why the big hurry, now that you're deceased?"

"I don't mean just about me, sir. There's a lot more. Stuff with the kids. Especially with Caroline. With all due respect, it's liable to kill her, sir. She won't understand, she doesn't see it coming. Somebody's gotta be there for her. Otherwise, it's just . . . well, it's just not—"

"Fair, Candidate Chance? There are a great many things you're not taking into consideration, here."

"But I see things I didn't see then, sir. I know things—about Harriet, about Caroline—things I had no way of knowing then."

"Had you looked a little harder, you might have at least suspected them, Candidate."

"I gotta go back."

"Out of the question."

"What if I don't comply?"

"Excuse me?"

"What will happen to me if I go down there again?"

"First, I'd say you better check your coordinates. That is, if you're heading *down* anywhere. '*Over* there' might be a little more accurate but still insufficient. '*In* there' is probably the closest."

"You know what I mean, sir. What will happen?"

"If you go rogue?"

"Yeah."

"Let's just say there are measures in place. It's not so different from your marines, Major. Think AWOL."

"But what will happen? Will it affect them?"

Charmichael redoubles his meaningful gaze. "In a word, Candidate Chance: nothing. Nothing will happen."

"I see, sir."

"To you, that is, Candidate. Nothing will happen to you. Things will still happen. Just not to you. Do we have an understanding?"

"Uh, yessir. I believe we do, sir."

"Good, then. Consider yourself warned."

"Yessir. I will."

"As you were," says Charmichael, waving him off. "And, Candidate?"

"Yessir?"

"The salute is unnecessary."

"Yessir."

April 16, 1959
(HARRIET AT TWENTY-TWO)

Mrs. Bernard Chance, it has a certain ring to it. Anyway, it's only a name—perhaps not the name you intended to make for yourself. But this is not your identity we're talking about, this is a logical step. A practical one. This isn't about your independence, this is about the rest of your life. This is about fulfillment. The kind of fulfillment no job can offer, at least not the jobs available to you. You knew from the start you'd never be a lawyer or a judge. You were destined for an administrative role. So, why not marriage? It turns out, your independence, like your salary, had a ceiling all along.

Besides, you're pregnant.

Oh, but don't despair, Harriet. Stolid, capable Bernard, whether he knows it or not, is willing. And he's a man who knows a thing or two about duty. About commitment and sacrifice, plumbing and electricity. And he's not a man who asks a lot of questions.

Just think, a spring wedding in Seattle, at the Rainier Club! Indoors, thank God, because yep, you guessed it, it's raining pitchforks. The parking lot is a lake. The awnings are sagging. But nothing can dampen your spirits today.

You're a gorgeous bride, Harriet—it's true, look at the pictures. In your mother's champagne-beaded dress, with the V-neck bodice, you cut an hourglass figure. You lost fifteen pounds starving yourself for this day. What's more, you're showing no outward signs of that little life taking hold inside of you, but it's there, you can feel it, the promise of fulfillment glowing in your cheeks.

Let's be honest, you're marrying down, as they say, a state of affairs that your mother will frequently remind you of in years to come. You're marrying a man who would sooner pick up a bowling ball than brandish a club or a racket. Though he had other plans for you, your father does not begrudge your decision to marry a janitor. At least he's a damn good janitor. No, your father has spared no expense on the wedding. The arrangements are elegant, perfectly tasteful. Everybody but everybody is there. People you don't know or can't place. Charlie Fitzsimmons is there. The *Times* runs a lavish paid announcement for the daughter of prominent attorney and local dignitary, Harriman Nathan.

You can already smell the shrimp puffs as the procession

gathers in the wings and the organ sounds its note. You've never been surer about anything, Harriet. Not that you haven't overcome a few nagging reservations over the past year. But you've managed to paint an idyllic picture of domestic life for yourself. It all starts with a honeymoon in Niagara Falls. A tiny house of your own in Seattle's north end, paid for with your own money, just you and Bernard. And baby makes three. Just think, this very Christmas, you'll hang those stockings. But let's not get ahead of ourselves again.

Your esteemed father, eyes misting as he leads you up the aisle, voice faltering as he gives you away, whispers to you that he could not be prouder. And there, beside you at the altar, is a man who knows what he wants, a man who speaks his mind and demands his just. A man who served his country. A man who has a center, whether it's moral or habitual. A man who vows to honor and protect you, in sickness and in health. To have and hold you, to love you and cherish you, from this day forward, for better or for worse, for richer, for poorer, until death do you part.

Yes, Harriet, for the next fifty years you'll eat what Bernard eats, vote how Bernard votes, love how Bernard loves, and ultimately learn to want out of life what Bernard wants out of life. Together you will see sickness and health. At times he will honor you. Occasionally, he will cherish you. Always he will protect you. But again, we get ahead of ourselves.

Right now, Harriet Nathan, that is, Harriet Chance, you are a beautiful bride.

August 13, 2015
(HARRIET AT SEVENTY-EIGHT)

Of course, Bernard's still alive in her imagination—that's only natural. Of course, she never heats the house above sixty-four degrees. Force of habit. Five decades of familiarity imprinted on her memory like a phantom limb. And yes, she still talks to him. These one-way conversations at the breakfast nook, or in bed, or while she's rummaging through the junk drawer in search of a screwdriver have been a small comfort the past nine months.

But an actual physical presence, one that talked back, this could be problematic. How long before it happens in public?

Hectored by these thoughts, Harriet trundles her grocery cart ever so deliberately down the cereal aisle toward the All-Bran, her arthritic spine burning like fire and ice. Her shopping is light: an overripe cantaloupe, her calcium supplement, a quart of skim milk, three Eating Right single-serve entrees (including her favorite, beef portobello). Just enough to last her until the cruise.

Short as her list is, the grocery cart proves to be a burden. What, with its wobbly front wheel spinning uselessly on its axis, a quarter inch above the white tile, an imprecision that surely would have driven Bernard into a state of muttering contempt, all the more so because the ball bearings themselves, those stalwarts of angular contact, those silent bearers of axial loads, to whose manufacture and distribution the Major had devoted twenty-eight years of his professional life, are rattling around like so many marbles inside the wheel assembly.

"They couldn't even get that right."

"Shhh," says Harriet, looking around the cereal aisle. "Not here!"

"Christ, if they'd just fit the damn bearings to the races properly."

"Bernard, shush! Don't make a scene."

"Well, it's like nobody gives a damn anymore. It's all about saving a nickel."

"Dear, your acid indigestion."

"Reflux! They call it reflux, now. Indigestion wasn't good enough!"

How many of these childish outbursts has Harriet endured over the course of the decades? Apparently, even death can't stop them. Do they embarrass her? Yes, often. Do they try her patience? Yes, frequently. But the truth is, if only covertly, Harriet has agreed with Bernard's grievances on nearly every count from lawn mowers, to stereo receivers, to family values—everything just seems to get worse. It's true: they really don't make them like they used to.

"Look, I'm sorry," he says. "I'm falling back into the same old patterns."

Harriet looks up and down the aisle again. "Please, Bernard, not here."

"Okay, fine," he says. "But I'll be back. We need to talk."

The question still burrowing like a wood beetle inside Harriet's brain is: Why? Why won't Bernard go away? Why has he come back to move his slippers around the house and complain about shoddy workmanship? The conventional wisdom suggests matters unresolved, but Harriet has neither the courage nor the inclination to further contemplate her failures.

Though it's barely 10:30 a.m., already she's exhausted. The weight of the impending cruise sits on her shoulders, a heavy dread. If only she could cancel without breaking Mildred's heart. From the beginning, Harriet hoped that Mildred would decline, so she wouldn't have to go herself, but she should have known better. This is Mildred we're talking about. She's been counting the days since June.

Of course Harriet wants to honor Bernard, but a cruise? All that activity, the lack of familiar routine. All that newness.

The mere thought of it is terrifying. Meanwhile, she may be losing her mind. Thank heavens she has her best friend to lean on. Mildred is a rock.

At the stand, the straw-haired checker with the flinty manner clutches Harriet's Val-U-Pack coupons with white knuckles, unable to suppress a sigh. The line is stacking up into the aisle, and Harriet knows it. But for the life of her, she can't find that five-dollar rebate from July's circular. More and more frequently of late, she's misplacing things. Car keys, recipes, thank-you notes. And, if she's to believe Father Mullinix, slippers and WD-40. Hands a-tremble, she burrows around fruitlessly in her purse. She's sure she put the voucher in the side pocket.

"Oh dear," she says, fishing out her reading glasses. "I know it's here."

"Uuugh," somebody groans near the back of the line.

"Tell me about it," whispers somebody else. "Should have seen this one coming, right?"

Just when Harriet is about to abandon her search, she realizes she's already clutching the voucher.

"Oh, here it is!" she says brightly, extending the coupon. "Silly me."

Snatching it from her liver-spotted hand, the checker inspects it. "Um, this expired eight days ago."

"You're sure?"

"It says so right here: expires eight five fourteen. See: Eight . . . five . . . fourteen."

It's not just her children—the whole world is convinced she's an idiot, benignly oblivious to the world around her, incapable of self-consciousness.

"Club Card?" says the checker.

"Oh yes," says Harriet, unclasping her purse again. "Let's see . . ."

Another groan from the back of the line, where a prematurely balding fellow with a five-o'clock shadow begins tapping his sandal anxiously on the floor. Harriet feels her face flushing. For heaven's sake, what's this young man's big hurry, anyway? He doesn't look particularly busy to Harriet. Really, what kind of grown man walks around wearing cutoff jeans and sandals on a workday? Bernard would have a field day.

"Would you like help out today?"

Harriet straightens herself up. "I can manage, thank you."

The checker eyes her doubtfully. "Let me get Chad. Chad!" she calls.

Soon, her long-suffering associate, a stout, slump-shouldered boy with an enormous brow ridge and perpetually chapped lips, assumes his post at the butt end of the checkout stand, where he pauses for a long moment, awaiting instructions, mouth agape, nose running.

"Can you help this young lady out?"

Chad gazes blankly, first at the checker, then at Harriet, before licking his ravaged lips.

While Harriet finds the boy quite agreeable, she prefers it when Chad does not bag her groceries. For, in the five years that Chad has been handling Harriet's groceries, the young man has not proven particularly adept at this charge, nor has he improved markedly over time—routinely stacking canned goods atop bread loaves, and crushing eggs beneath melons. Still, Harriet has always known the young man to be quite helpful in other respects: remembering daylight savings, for instance, reminding her to set her clock back. As far as Harriet can tell, he is under no obligation from Safeway, or anyone else, to do so. In an age of paranoia and declining social niceties, Harriet finds Chad refreshingly forthcoming, not only with his reminders but also with his personal observations. Such as the fact that he likes cats. Or that his aunt has eight of them. Or that one of them is named Stuart. Indeed, the young man is quite personable in light of—or perhaps because of—his condition.

"Earth to Chad," says the checker.

As Harriet and Chad inch their way across the crowded lot, the boy seems uncharacteristically reserved. It's not raining, yet Chad has failed to comment on the lack of rain. Has he sensed her low opinion of his work? She's relieved when he finally breaks his silence.

"My birthday is June 23," he observes.

"Well, that's nice, dear."

"When were you born?"

"November the sixth, darling."

"What year?"

Harriet can feel herself blushing again. She can't possibly hold the child responsible for such a gaff.

"Dear, that's an impolite question. But if you must know, the answer is 1936."

My God, it sounds impossible. Harriet has outlasted climates. She's on geological time. And yet, daily, she feels the minutes of her life grinding slowly to a standstill. The sight of the Olds is just one more reminder of her shrinking existence.

Skip is even firmer than Caroline on the subject of driving. Last year, he almost ruined Thanksgiving for Harriet with his exhortations.

"Look, Mom, it's nothing personal," he assured her in the kitchen as she basted and stirred and boiled. "This is about your condition."

"Osteoarthritis?"

"No, age," he said with a mouthful of deviled egg. "I'm sorry, Mom, but eighty is just too old to drive—"

"Seventy-eight."

"I'm just saying, there's a law that says you can't drive before a certain age, and there ought to be one that says you can't drive *after* a certain age. You've got a busted taillight and a chipmunk plastered to your wheel. And what happened to that rear-side panel? Did you hit something?"

Harriet averted her attention to the gravy.

"Not a pedestrian, I hope?"

"Good heavens, no! A shopping cart. And it hit me, Skip!"

As it happened, the cart really hadn't been Harriet's fault. Come to think of it, it had probably been Chad's fault. He was supposed to wheel the cart back—not leave it sitting there in her blind spot (on an incline, no less!). Still, Harriet can hardly blame the poor dear. The least she can do, though, is gently remind him, this time.

"Chad, dear," she says as he slams the trunk closed, licking his lips. "Could you please remember to wheel the cart back?"

September 11, 1988
(HARRIET AT FIFTY-ONE)

Yes, we're getting ahead of ourselves again, but hey, it happens, Harriet. The reflective mind is a pinball, pitching and careening, rebounding off anything it makes contact with. Really, how can we not think of Mildred at this juncture? As always, you're counting on her.

Mildred Honeycutt, ever your savior, and right from the start.

Here you are, Harriet, in the airless basement of St. Luke's on that scorcher of a Sunday so long ago, nervous, reluctant, miserable, as your poor, untouched Bundt cake all but collapses under its own weight in the stultifying heat. Thank heavens for Mildred Honeycutt, with her cropped hair and bold, disarming nature, not only for extending a welcome on behalf of the entire congregation but for having the courage and politeness to wash two slices of your disastrous confection down with her weak coffee.

You are taken immediately by Mildred Honeycutt. And let's face it, her attentiveness has everything to do with it. At fifty-one, you feel overlooked. You never thought you'd miss that licentious slap on the fanny. But twenty-nine years of rigorous routine and loyal service to your family have made a wallflower of you, Harriet, or that's what you think, anyway.

Look at the way Mildred blushes as she pours your coffee. Why, she can hardly look at you. And yet, when she thinks you're not looking, she can't seem to take her eyes off of you. She makes you feel fascinating. Admired. Mysterious.

How long has it been since you've had a friend—your own friend? Not Margaret Blum but a trusted confidante. Yes, Harriet, you long for companionship outside of Bernard's influence. Somebody to commiserate with. Somebody you can complain to. Somebody to listen to you without offering advice. How is it that you've so rarely managed to achieve this? Why is female fellowship forever so elusive to you? Are you different from other women?

In the early going, Mildred vexes you somewhat with her impalpable nature, even as she tempts you with familiarity. You sense she wants more of you, and yet she is not solicitous of intimacy. But there's something at work beneath the surface of her that draws you to Mildred. You exchange recipes and benign commentary. The sermon, the humidity, the fading lavender. She never mentions her husband, but that diamond must be four karats. Likewise, she never inquires about Bernard, or your children, or your home. You reason that Mildred Honeycutt is shyer than you gave her credit for, that her boldness is a tool meant to deflect, and this makes you want to know her more.

Not until Week 3, when you serve together at the All Hallow's Eve dinner downtown, does Mildred finally surrender.

"Have you ever been horseback riding?" she asks.

And like that, your friendship is off at a canter.

Look at you, at Lost Mountain Ranch, atop your shimmering mount! At any rate, look at you, atop that spindly-legged nag with the lackluster coat and the respiratory problems. Still, you feel big in the saddle, with all that power beneath you. Bigger than you've felt in years. And you have Mildred Honeycutt to thank for it.

You will have many things to thank Mildred for in the years to come. Mildred will offer you everything in the way of female fellowship you ever yearned for. She will listen and absorb, consider you without judgment. She will push you and guide you and test you. But none of it will happen overnight. No, Mildred is a safe that requires cracking.

The week after your adventure at Lost Mountain Ranch, without explanation, Mildred leaves St. Luke's, for good, though she remains your friend for many years to come.

Though Harriet doesn't dare confide as much to Mildred, she finds the subtropical artifice of Sunny Acres odious in most respects—the potted palms, the bougainvillea, the thatched-roofed utility sheds. The housekeepers in their white aprons, the attendants (invariably Hispanic or black) zipping around in golf carts, tipping their hats as they whir past. All of it feels like a resort to Harriet and, by extension, a lie.

Sunny Acres promotes health and active living, but it nurtures dependence. Oh, there are origami classes and whirlpools, to be sure. But these aren't the sort of activities that keep a person vital. Raking leaves keeps you vital. Paying bills, running errands. For all its pretension, Harriet knows that

Sunny Acres is priced competitively. Otherwise, Mildred's son, Dwight, would've sequestered her somewhere more affordable.

Mildred greets Harriet at the curb in front of her unit, which smells of pill jars and candle wax. She stands, all five feet of her, in a long and unseasonably warm pistachio-colored double-knit jacket of some vintage; one hand rests on her aluminum walker.

"You just missed Dwight," she observes.

"Mmm," says Harriet, crossing her arms in front of her.

"He said to say hello."

Harriet gazes off in the direction of the pool house. Mildred dusts the lapel of her coat, then fidgets irritably with her hair.

"Oh, you're just a paranoid old bag of bones, you know that? And quit equating this place with Sherwood Arms. This is *not* Sherwood Arms. And what happened with Bernard was no fault of yours. You know darn well, it's not as if I'm under lock and key, here. You think Dwight dragged me here kicking and screaming, but the truth is I was tired, darling. That big house was too much for me. All those stairs. All that lawn. I've explained all of this before, dear. You just don't want to hear it."

"Hmph," says Harriet.

"Well, it's true," Mildred insists. "At some point, you just get tired of hanging on. All those memories. All that junk."

If nothing else, it's heartening to hear Mildred defend herself. Lately, her spunky self-assurance, her fizzy good humor, her bubbly optimism, her signature Monday morning effervescence—they're all flattening like warm soda.

"I apologize for the wait," says Mildred, checking her watch. "Fikru should be here any minute. Perhaps he's having trouble with his cart."

"I'm in no hurry," says Harriet. "Why don't we walk?"

As if on cue, Fikru whizzes up on his golf cart with a clownish little honk of the horn and comes to a stop directly in front of them.

"'Allo, ladies," he says with a toothsome smile and a tip of his hat.

Fikru hails from Ethiopia. Or maybe Kenya. Harriet's ashamed of her geographical ignorance every time she sees the young man.

"You are looking exquisite today, Ms. Harriet. Your beauty has an expansive quality to it, like the savanna after the rainy season."

Harriet blanches. She sees these flirtations for exactly what they are, of course: hospitalities. And yet she cherishes the attention. If she felt overlooked at fifty, she feels downright invisible at seventy-eight.

"And you, Ms. Mildred," Fikru croons, stepping down from his cart, where he makes a wafting gesture with his hand, breathing deeply. "Fragrant as the Abyssinian rose."

As Fikru assists Mildred into the backseat of the cart, stowing her walker in the front passenger's seat, Harriet awaits her turn with mounting anticipation. When the young man returns to offer his assistance, Harriet is standing as upright as possible, elbow at the ready.

"You have a spritelike step, Ms. Harriet," he notes, leading her up the cart.

Yes, Fikru is laying it on thick this afternoon. Perhaps he senses that Harriet's opinion of Sunny Acres is softening. Maybe he gets a commission. Still, Harriet settles into her seat with the tiniest of flutters in her chest as Fikru resumes his station behind the wheel and taps the horn again.

"Hold on tight, ladies, while I deliver you."

Harriet is still under the influence of Fikru's considerable charm as they wend their way through Sunny Acres, maneuvering between colonnades of potted palms and meticulous lawns, cut through with gently winding concrete paths, everywhere the trilling of chipmunks. With her best friend seated beside her, Harriet tries to convince herself she could get used to the lifestyle. Perhaps she'd been judging the place harshly. Perhaps after all the gas-inducing anxiety of this surprise cruise, she'll take a shine to the palliative environs of Sunny Acres: the hypnotic whir of the golf carts, the rhythmic spitting of sprinkler heads. The hint of the tropics clinging to the gentle breeze. Surely, a body could do worse than Sunny Acres. But no sooner does Harriet embrace this inclination than she turns to see Bernard seated beside her.

"Sounds like a place they send horses to die. And what is it with these damn golf carts buzzing around everywhere like mosquitoes? The place can't be but three acres."

Harriet shushes him. "Go on now, get. Not here. You can't just pop up anytime you feel like expressing an opinion, Bernard. People are going to think I'm crazy."

"Well?"

"And don't sulk."

"Who's sulking?"

"Go," she says.

Fikru turns in the driver seat, wearing a big pearly grin. "Everything is okay, Miss Harriet?"

"Yes, just fine, dear."

By the time they reach the clubhouse, where they whir to a halt between two guard rails, their chariot has begun to feel like a pumpkin again. Even Fikru's charm has lost some of its luster as he assists them off the cart. Beneath his magnanimous air, he now strikes Harriet as a tad too efficient, a tad too curt and professional in his movements, a tad too quick to hop back into the cart and give a honk, as if, indeed, he has delivered them, as a postman might deliver a package.

"Isn't this convenient?" says Mildred.

As they begin the thirty-foot trek to the front door of the clubhouse, Harriet can't help but notice that Mildred is depending on her walker more than ever. The past couple years have not been kind to Mildred's health. She's shrinking before Harriet's eyes.

Nothing about the clubhouse—not the low ceiling, nor the hospital-like sterility, nor the smell of Glade air freshener—inspires Harriet's appetite. With the dining room to themselves, they agree on a table by the window, overlooking the guest parking lot, which Harriet notices is also conspicuously empty, save for her own Oldsmobile.

"Try something new today, darling," Mildred urges. "The Szechuan chicken is delightful. Not too spicy."

Is it going to be like this all cruise long, Harriet wonders, Mildred presiding over Harriet's every dietary choice? Yes, Harriet has always liked that Mildred nudged, cajoled, and even forced her to venture beyond her safe boundaries. Without Mildred's encouragement, Harriet might never have known the joys of slot machines, Qigong massage, or cross-country skiing. She appreciates it, truly she does. It's just that, well, sometimes Mildred can be a little pushy, though Harriet feels guilty even thinking as much.

But for Pete's sake, there's something to be said for a little consistency. That's what drew her toward Bernard in the first place—consistency, predictability, a propensity toward repetition. Harriet likes her routines, she enjoys her frozen beef portobello, her chicken Caesars. Her system is accustomed to them—their uniform size and agreeable texture, their stable calorie count. With few exceptions—most recently, the cruise—Harriet sees little reason to diverge from her routines, most particularly with regard to diet.

The waitress soon arrives for their orders. Mildred orders the crab melt with a side salad—one of the specials. Harriet doesn't stray from her customary Caesar.

Mildred remains all but silent through lunch, to the point where Harriet wonders if perhaps she isn't having one of her spells. Finally, she inquires as much.

"Oh no, I'm fine, darling," Mildred assures her.

"Good, then. Let's get started."

The moment the waitress clears their plates and wipes the table clean, Harriet dons her reading glasses and spreads out her cruise materials on the tabletop. Highlighter poised, she begins their weekly exercise.

"Okay. Thursday at ten thirty a.m. Let's see, we have the Greenhouse Spa & Salon raffle in the Lido spa or the Good-feet Clinic—I'm leaning toward the foot clinic."

After a moment of silence, Harriet glances up from her planner at Mildred, who has yet to ready her materials.

"So sorry, dear," says Harriet. "Have I jumped the gun again?"

Mildred casts her eyes down, then piles her hands in her lap.

"Are you sure you're okay, dear? You look a little peaked."

"Oh, darling, I just can't do it anymore," Mildred proclaims.

"I'm overplanning, aren't I?" says Harriet, setting her checklist and pen on the tabletop. "Oh, I'm sorry, dear, I know it's aggravating, it's Bernard. He was always so damn insistent upon—"

"That's not what I mean."

"It's the Celebrity Cook-Off in the Culinary Arts Center, isn't it?"

Mildred reaches a trembling hand out and clutches Harriet's. "Darling, I can't go on pretending."

"Pretending?"

"I've known for weeks. I just couldn't stand the idea of disappointing you. I just thought if I . . ."

"Mildred, what are you talking about?"

"The cruise, darling."

"You're absolutely right. Let's not overdo it."

"I can't do it, darling, I can't go."

It takes a moment for the realization to settle in.

"Well, dear, are you all right?" Harriet hears herself saying. "Is this a health issue?"

Mildred casts her gaze out on the empty lot. "Oh, darling, please don't let's talk about my reasons. Just think, you can go to the Goodfeet Clinic. You can skip the mixology class. And I won't make you try sushi. You can do anything you please without me browbeating you. And surely you'll meet all kinds of nice people."

Classic Mildred. Another inexplicable decision. Like leaving the church three weeks after they met. Like canceling the couples' retreat two years in a row. Like cutting her hair off, buying a horse, renouncing wheat and cosmetics. Here was the Achilles' heel of their friendship, and Harriet's lone misgiving with Mildred, this maddening capacity to surprise those around her, and without explanation.

"Well, I don't know what to say, Mildred."

"Oh, Harriet, don't say anything. I didn't want it to be this way, please understand."

"Is Dwight behind this?"

"Darling, no. It's complex."

That's it? It's complex? That's all she's got in the way of an explanation? With trembling hands, Harriet begins gathering her cruise materials, then stands and walks out of the clubhouse, leaving Mildred behind.

"Forgive me, please," Mildred calls out.

The moment Harriet hits the open air, clutching the guard rail, it shames her to find that she feels nothing so much as relief. She's off the hook. No cruise! No mixers, no seminars, no raw fish!

"So, that's it, you're not going?" It's Bernard again.

"You don't honestly expect me to go alone?"

"Take one of the kids," says Bernard.

"You know that's not going to happen."

"Couldn't hurt to ask."

"Well, it wouldn't do any good, either."

"What about Barbara Chatsworth, then?"

"She's in poor health—hospitalized last month, the poor dear. Besides, I think I grate on her nerves."

"Well, how about somebody else from the church? That little Higashi lady that makes the cobblers?"

Harriet sighs. "It really means that much to you?"

"I didn't say that. I just think you oughta get out and live a little, Harriet. Be adventurous."

"Why should I start now?"

"You deserve it. Now that you haven't got me to lug around, you owe yourself a little vacation."

"Oh, Bernard, I just don't understand. You know I'm terrible on boats. I can hardly bear the ferry to Edmonds. Why did you bid on an Alaskan cruise, for heaven's sake? Why not a basket of artisan breads?"

He shrugs.

"Well, if you wanted to surprise me, you succeeded in that."

She reaches out for his hand and gives it a little squeeze.

When she arrives at the straightaway path leading to the visitors' lot, she hears the clownish little honk and the whir of the motor and turns just in time to find Fikru coasting to a stop beside her, beaming like a jack-o'-lantern.

"'Allo, Ms. Harriet!" he says, pocketing his cell phone. "Have you lost your way?"

"Gracious, no."

"May I deliver you?"

"No, thank you, dear," Harriet says. "I'll handle my own deliverance, thank you very much."

December 22, 1959
(HARRIET AT TWENTY-THREE)

While there's only so much you can do to fudge the math, nobody makes an issue of bouncing baby Skipper's arrival, seven and a half months after your wedding day. And just in time for Christmas! You've got what you wanted, Harriet: stockings festooning your hearth. And you got a lot more in the bargain, too: a colicky infant who doesn't sleep and never stops filling diapers, a ruined figure, a husband who's never home. You've got endless nights in steamy bathrooms and endless days of domestic toil. Somehow, though it seems impossible, you didn't see this coming. Suddenly your life is filled with talcum and baby oil and laundry soap. Pee and poop and spit-up. Tide, Wisk, Cheer, you've tried them all—yes, even All! You've tried reading magazines while Skip is napping, even television. But nothing seems to whisk away the tide of despair. Nothing seems to cheer you. All of it is futile.

Filing deposition notices suddenly doesn't look so bad next to the tedium of homemaking. Drafting court appeals was never this thankless. And this is nothing compared to what you'll endure with Caroline. When you get a moment's leisure, you're cagey. Just look at you, Harriet, pacing the house, displacing pillows, rearranging furniture. Looking for purpose. When all else fails, you go shopping.

Yearning to be noticed, you experiment with hairstyles, cinch your waist with fitted jumpers, and when that doesn't work, you starve yourself. Look at you, with your plate of turnips. And, by God, it works! Your figure returns! But nobody seems to notice, not the butcher, not even Bernard.

But like everything else, it's only going to get worse, Harriet. Within three months, Bernard will be around even less, landing a job as plant manager at Blum Bearing, where he often works two shifts. When he comes home exhausted, he takes a mild interest in the child for about ten minutes, eats the warmed-over dinner you've set before him, and then hides behind his newspaper for the rest of the evening.

In bed, he turns his back to you, and you wonder what you've done.

You understand the pressure he's under, the weight of responsibility he must feel. And yet you're powerless to share this responsibility. The best you can do is pick a good melon and keep the linoleum clean, launder his work clothes, and stock the refrigerator. Depleting as they are, these accomplishments feel empty.

Oh, but let's not forget the joys of domesticity, Harriet! Here you are, decked out in curlers and a terry-cloth bathrobe with baby Skipper in the ER shortly after he swallowed the paper clip. You berate yourself for being a useless mother, who can't even keep her child out of the hospital. All you can do is scour his poopy diapers for the next three days, looking for the offending object.

And here you are again, in the same bathrobe and curlers, consulting with firefighters who have responded to your frantic call regarding the smoking Maytag. Five armored giants rush into your laundry room with axes only to return minutes later, slightly deflated. Turns out, the machine is simply overworked.

This is your life, Harriet, what it's become.

But do not lose heart. Things will get better after the first year: Skip will hit his sleeping stride, start taking the bottle, the colic will subside, you'll find a reliable babysitter in Cindy Blum. Bernard will take a full week off next Christmas. But by then, Fourth and Union, and the joys of your former life, will already seem a long ways away. That other Harriet, the self-realized one, has gone on without you.

August 13, 2015
(HARRIET AT SEVENTY-EIGHT)

When Harriet arrives home from Sunny Acres, she's thrilled to discover Skip's silver SUV in the driveway in spite of the fact that it's parked perilously close to her dahlias. She thinks guiltily of the creased fender, for which Skip—like his father, a zealous maintainer—will surely expect an accounting.

Halfway up the drive, Harriet's stomach tightens as she spots Caroline peering out the kitchen window. Smiling stiffly, Harriet issues a little wave. Suddenly, her thoughts are racing. What will she make for lunch? Does she have time to bake something? She hopes the living room isn't a mess. Sandwiches, she can make sandwiches. They can eat outside on the patio! Maybe they'll stay the night. Oh, what a surprise!

She finds Skip in the living room in front of the TV, eating dill pickles straight from the jar. Snapping off the television, he swings his feet off the coffee table and sets the remote aside.

"Hello, dear, what a surprise!" she says.

He walks to the kitchen and bends down to hug her. At fifty-five, with flecks of gray marking his wavy hair above the ears, he still manages to look boyish in his purple UW hat and running shoes.

"Hello, dear," she says to Caroline, who makes no move to hug her.

At forty-eight, with sallow cheeks and scarecrow hair, Caroline looks like Skip's elder by at least five years.

"What are you two doing here? I had no idea!"

We thought we'd pop by for a visit," says Skip. "We both had the day off, so we figured, you know, let's drop in on Mom."

"How wonderful! Oh, but I do wish you would have called ahead, dear, so I could prepare something. Let me make you a sandwich."

"Nah, it's all right, Ma, I just had a few pickles. I'm good."

"Caroline, honey, let me make you a sandwich. You look so thin."

"Gee, thanks, Mom. You always know how to make me feel good about myself."

"Honey, I didn't mean it like that. C'mon, I'll set up the patio. I do hope you're staying the night? We can rent a DVD!"

"Look, Mom," says Skip. "The thing is, we didn't just pop by for a visit."

"Oh," says Harriet, crestfallen. "You mean, you're not staying?"

"We can't, Mom."

"Surely you can at least stay for dinner?"

"Mom," says Skip. "I got a call last night from Father Mulligan."

"*Mullinix*, dear. Where on earth did he get your number?"

"He told Skip about the phantom WD-40," says Caroline, lowering herself into Bernard's recliner.

Skip sits down on the sofa, and immediately leans forward. "He said you were acting really strange, Mom. He was worried."

Harriet feels herself blush, at once from embarrassment and irritation. "I was exhausted," she says. "I served downtown all day at the prayer station. There's no air-conditioning down there. Did Father Mullinix tell you that? I was overheated. But I'm perfectly fine now, I assure you."

It comforts her to know that Skip genuinely worries about her.

"Mom," he says. "We're just concerned. He said you thought you had dinner with dad at the Bon Marche."

"Frederick and Nelson."

"Right. Frederick and Nelson." Skip doffs his cap, runs a hand through his thick hair. "Mom, Frederick and Nelson closed twenty years ago! I don't even think that old buffet did dinners."

"I saw him, Skip, with my own eyes. I touched him."

"Mom, I had a dream my hands were made of soap. But look, they're not!" He submits his outthrust hands as evidence.

"It's not the same thing."

"It is, Mom. It was a dream."

"No. It wasn't."

"Okay, what then? A hallucination?"

"Not exactly," says Harriet.

"Whatever it was, Mom, it has nothing to do with reality."

"Fine, maybe it doesn't mean anything. There, are you satisfied? But just suppose I took a little comfort in it, how about that? Well, then, I suppose you two would want to deprive me of that, wouldn't you?"

"Mom, that's not how it is," Skip insists, fishing a fresh pickle from the jar. "What have we deprived you of?"

"He's right," says Caroline. "We're just concerned about your well-being."

"Oh, stop Caroline. Like you were concerned with your father's well-being?"

"Mom," Skip says. "This is different. Dad was incapacitated."

"He's reaching out," says Harriet. "Don't you see? That's what this is about. I've been thinking long and hard about it, and I'm sure he's come to help. Maybe to guide me."

"Let's hope not," says Skip.

"That would be a first," mutters Caroline.

"What is that supposed to mean?"

"It means he was never much help while he was alive."

"Take that back, Caroline."

"Oh, c'mon, Mom. You did everything. You cleaned, you

cooked, you did every single thing he ever told you to do. The Major just sat around polishing his belt buckles and reading newspapers."

Though Harriet appreciates the affirmation, it annoys her that she should have to defend a protocol designed specifically to eradicate obstacles for her children. Why should Harriet apologize when she tended to every runny nose and broken bone, prepared every meal, consoled every heartbreak and disappointment, all so that Caroline and Skip could enjoy a better quality of life than her own? It breaks Harriet's heart that Caroline squandered every opportunity, that she sabotaged her life with bad decisions. It breaks her heart that Caroline never gave her grandchildren and that Caroline's unofficial "foster daughter" is, and always has been, something of a problem, much like Caroline herself. But what breaks Harriet's heart the most is that things might have been different. She might have saved Caroline. Or Bernard, for that matter.

"That doesn't change the fact that he was your father," says Harriet. "Or that I failed him."

"He was a bully, Mom. Quit saying you failed him. You were his servant, his nurse, you were practically his mother. The only meal Dad could cook was toast."

"And beans," says Harriet.

"Fine, and beans. I mean, who gets to be ninety years old and never cooks a single meal for himself besides beans and toast?"

"He made tapioca pudding, too. Oh, Caroline dear. I know

you had your differences. But you're nearly fifty years old. Isn't it time to forgive your father?"

"Why, because you did?"

"I fell apart, Caroline."

"He's the one who fell apart."

"C'mon, you guys," says Skip, brandishing his pickle like a traffic wand. "We're not getting anywhere here."

"Where are we supposed to be getting to? Is this another intervention?"

"Settle down, Mom."

"You vacuumed under some sofa cushions at your father's wake. You made a few calls to the insurance company. But when did I ever ask either of you for help? Darlings, if you really want to help me, fix that garage door, and pressure-wash those steps. Clean the gutters. If you want to comfort me, how about sending an Easter card? Or reminding my grandchildren that I exist?"

Caroline looks away.

"Okay, Mom," says Skip. "I get it."

Skip takes Harriet's elbow and leads her the first few steps to the sofa. Halfway there, she breaks free.

"My goodness, a few phone calls, a couple trips to the dump—that's all I ever asked."

"Mom," says Skip. "The thing is, look: we just think this cruise is too much right now. Caroline, back me up here. We really think you ought to call Mildred and postpone the thing. Maybe in a few months, when—"

"Absolutely not," Harriet says, surprising herself. "I intend to honor your father, no matter what the two of you might think of him. He bought this cruise for me; he intended it for the two of us, the least I can do is go on the darn thing. And I'm taking his ashes with me."

"Mom, is that even legal?"

"Don't try to talk me out of this, Skip."

"But Mom, you—"

"Please. Let me do this."

Her children exchange glances. Caroline shrugs.

"And Mildred, she's good to go?" says Skip.

"Yes," lies Harriet. She knows it may be her only chance.

"You'll take it easy, right?" he says. "Promise?"

"I promise."

Skip looks to Caroline for approval.

"Why are you looking at me?" she says.

September 8, 1962
(HARRIET AT TWENTY-FIVE)

Then, after a few wearisome years of domestic drudgery, a few years sequestered in your little house, in your little neighborhood, with your little problems, something happens. The outside world calls. On the north end of downtown, they've erected a futuristic wonderland, a marvelous, humming other-world full of possibilities, punctuated by a six hundred foot exclamation point. It's impossible not to get caught up in the excitement. Suddenly your life, by mere extension, does not seem so small.

Is that a smile, Harriet Chance?

Look at you, on the global stage! All the world is taking notice of you and your gorgeous city, drinking you up like a Sloe Gin Fizz. The traffic jams are horrific. The lines are soul-crushing. But there is magic at the end of each one.

There you are, Harriet, on the amazing Bubbleator, Skipper, nearly three years old, clutching your hand tightly, World's Fair lariat cinched securely around his neck, smiling up at you. At 130 pounds, you've never looked better. And look at Bernard, fit as ever, his arm, strong and able, around your waist, as the Bubbleator ascends into the unknown. The future is on everybody's mind, and you're on a rocket ship speeding toward middle age, but suddenly you're okay with that.

Maybe, like everyone else on the Bubbleator, you're no longer taking your future for granted. A single phone call, a little red button, and poof, it could all disappear. Have you finally embraced domestic life, Mrs. Bernard Chance? Have you released your independence at long last? Have you finally stopped tracking the progress of that other incarnation of yourself, the one who didn't bow to the expectations of society, the one who didn't opt for the easy way out, the one who wasn't going to have children until she was thirty?

Or have you simply lowered your standards?

It helps that Bernard has started to notice you again lately. He's showing signs of tenderness, displays of affection. Rarely does he pass you in the hallway or in the kitchen without some physical communication—the grazing of an elbow, the touch of a hand, and yes, even a pat on the fanny. What's more, he's taken an interest in Skip now that the boy can talk. Together, they go to the Montlake landfill on Sunday, where they sit in the Buick and eat BurgerMeister fries, marveling at the perfectly good things people throw away.

Perhaps it's that promotion to general manager that has put a little spring back in Bernard's step. Weekends, he's sporting a Hawaiian shirt, to which he attributes good fortune. If not a friend, you've found an amusement in Margaret Blum. On Friday nights, the four of you, Gene and Bernard, you and Margaret, dine together at the Blums' house in Madison Park. You play cards: pinochle, poker, bridge. You drink Zombies and Stingers and Pink Squirrels. And sometimes you surprise yourself with your candor and familiarity.

By the time you get home to release the sitter, you're already missing your little Skipper. Some Friday nights, you wobble to his room and listen to the excited sound of your own breathing in the darkness as you watch him sleep. You want to pick him up and hold him, caress the downy hair on the back of his neck. You want to wake him from his sleep, so you can hear the singsong of his little voice, so you can answer his thousand questions. There, there, that's all you needed, Harriet: a little space once in a while to decompress, a little time for abstraction, a little distance from which to count your blessings. And yes, a few Zombies never hurt.

If the hustle and bustle of Fourth and Union still seems a long ways off, so does the thankless malaise of last year.

It's the good life, Harriet Chance, drink it up!

August 19, 2015
(HARRIET AT SEVENTY-EIGHT)

'm so sorry to keep you waiting, dear," says Harriet, answering her doorbell the morning of the cruise. "Please come in. I'll just be a minute."

She's sorely misjudged Dwight Honeycutt, and the guilt of this miscalculation has been needling at her conscience for two days. All these years, Harriet's been looking at Dwight with a jaundiced eye. Yes, he was the chief proponent of Mildred's move to Sunny Acres, the liquidation of her automobile, the downsizing of her existence. Yes, he dresses like a fallen oil baron, in bolo ties and ten-gallon hats, cowboy boots with khaki dress suits. And then there's the matter of the silver Jaguar, out there in the driveway, crouched in the pink dawn, quietly belching a plume of exhaust into her dahlias. It's true he landed a tidy sum listing the bluff house. But why shouldn't he? It was going to be his someday, anyway. The truth is, all of it was probably in Mildred's best interest. Harriet can see that now.

Dwight has been a doll the past two days. He feels terrible that his mother has canceled. Yesterday he called to confirm the ride for the second time. He even offered to come over and take a look around the house, make sure everything was in working order. Not only that, he offered to house-sit, and pick up the mail in her absence. She feels terrible for underestimating him.

"Take your time, take your time," Dwight says, from the open kitchen, admiring the stainless-steel appliances, running a hand cleanly across the marble countertop. "You sure you don't need a hand?"

"No, no, dear. I'm almost ready."

It's no small kindness, Dwight's offering to drive Harriet as far as Kingston—and at 6:00 a.m., no less. That he was considerate enough to arrive twenty minutes ahead of schedule just puts a fine point on it.

No, there's nothing shifty about Dwight Honeycutt as he sashays from room to room, flipping light switches, turning water spigots on and off, knocking on walls, inquiring about square footage, admiring views, peering keenly out at the patio.

"Hot tub work?"

"As far as I know, dear. Bernard maintained it scrupulously."

"Nice amenity."

"I really ought to use it more, you're right."

The relative dryness of the banana belt, sheltered as it was by the rain shadow, had been the decisive selling point, when shortly after his retirement from Blum Bearing in '88, Bernard made the mutual decision that they were leaving the city for the peninsula. Oh, not that there hadn't been some discussion on the subject. Harriet's objections had been heard, among them not wanting to leave the kids (though Skip was nearly thirty), not wanting to sell the family home (though truth be told, it was a drafty old Edwardian with all the frigid corners of a haunted house), and not wanting to say good-bye to their friends (though, let's face it, how exciting did twenty more years of playing pinochle with Gene and Margaret Blum sound?). In the end, it was a game of inches. Only eighteen inches of precipitation annually in Sequim, according to the real estate agent. Nearly thirty inches less than Seattle. More than pollution, more than crime, traffic, high property taxes, or any symptom of urban decay, Bernard could not abide rust. A corrosive menace. An insidious predator.

"Gotta love this rain shadow," says Dwight, as though he can hear her thoughts. "No wonder everybody wants to retire here."

Harriet never wanted to leave the north end, it's true. She and Bernard had both been born and come of age in Seattle. They'd raised their children in the Ravenna house. But twenty-seven years later, hunched in the passenger's seat next to Dwight, Harriet thinks of Sequim as the place she's spent the best years of her life.

It all started with the house—the one decision over which Bernard had been willing to grant Harriet the final word. Because she saw to its upkeep, organization, and operation, the home and hearth would ever remain Harriet's domain. Long after Bernard had lost patience (having viewed a dozen listings and attended half as many open houses), Harriet was finally swept off her feet by a cedar-sided one-of-a-kind in the Carlsborg flats. It was everything the family house in Ravenna was not, with its river-rock chimney, spacious sunroom, and jetted tub in the master suite. The kitchen was a dream, airy and uncluttered, with counter space galore. She loved the cedar-scented charm of her new home. The luxurious sparsity of the open floor plan. There were even two darling guest rooms for the kids when they visited, and a rec room in the basement for the grandchildren (if Skip would hurry up and produce some). Out back, through the sliding glass double doors, lay a wide flagstone patio facing the Olympics, flanked on all sides by raised garden beds. And all of it for barely two-thirds of what they'd managed to get for the Ravenna house.

"Oh yeah," says Dwight, reaching for the glove box, from which he proffers a white envelope. "Mom said to wait until the cruise until you read it. And no, it's not money—I already checked."

The unmarked envelope is stuffed tight and sealed neatly.

"What's this? An explanation?"

"I can't honestly say. All I know is that she wanted you to wait."

In spite of an unhealthy curiosity, Harriet tucks the envelope neatly in the side pouch of her oversized purse. She turns her attention back to the scenery, which like virtually everything else in the modern world, seems to be changing too fast. Goodness, but how they've built up Sequim in the past ten years. The box stores, the hotels, the thoughtless housing developments spreading like gray rashes into the hills. Harriet can remember when there was practically nothing along this strip of Highway 101, she could remember Sequim before the bypass, when the banana belt was a rural outpost, an oddball menagerie of gutsy merchants, not the shopping hub of the peninsula. Fifteen years on, and she still thinks of it as the new highway.

"How is she?" Harriet says at last.

"Incorrigible, if you wanna know the truth."

"Her health, I mean. Is there something wrong she's not telling me about?"

"She's fine," he says. "Slowing down a bit. Getting a little finicky in her old age, no offense. Frankly, I have no idea why she flaked out on you like this. For years, she tried to get dad to take her to Alaska. But he was always too busy."

Dwight reaches for the console and cracks the sunroof with an electric whir. "There's a bottle of water in back if you want it."

"Thank you, dear, I'm fine."

"Anyway, I'm sorry about my mom," he says, notching his bolo tighter. "She could've given you a little warning. You've gotta understand, she's very needy these days, whether she wants to admit it or not. She can't drive, she can't hardly boil water without forgetting to turn the burner off. And she's getting loopier by the day. I'm afraid she's gonna get herself in trouble trying to do too much, you know? Probably a good thing she's not going."

"I do hope she's okay," says Harriet, feeling a pang of guilt.

"If you wanna worry about somebody, worry about me. I'm sixty years old, and I'm maxed. Beyond maxed. Upside down. I've re-fied twice in the past eighteen months. I don't even know how I'll make my mortgage next month without Mom's help. And this car—ha! I'm two payments behind already."

Dwight reaches for the glove box again, this time producing a small tin. Harriet's certain he's about to offer her a breath mint, when he opens the tin to reveal a number of hand-rolled marijuana cigarettes. Fishing a chrome lighter out of his coat pocket, he lights one of the joints and takes a long pull.

"You're all right, Harriet Chance," he says, holding his breath. Bobbing his eyebrows a few times, he offers her the joint.

"Good heavens, no."

Though Harriet does not approve of smoking grass (legal or not, in automobiles or anywhere else), she's forced to admit after ten minutes that the marijuana markedly improves Dwight's driving. Moreover, it seems to take the edge off his personality. He proves to be a delightful conversationalist. Whatever his habits are, whatever his past looks like, Harriet is forced once again to acknowledge her misjudgment of Dwight. She'll be sure to include an apology in her first postcard to Mildred, whom she finds herself unable to begrudge.

When he drops her at the curb, Dwight circles the car to assist her with her luggage. Extricating her wheelie bag from amid a jumble of real estate placards, he hefts it on the pavement and reaches for his wallet. For an instant, Harriet thinks he's going to offer her money. But instead, he presents her with a business card.

"Look," he says. "I appreciate the friend you've been to my mom—she appreciates it. You've always been there for her. I really wanna help. Anything I can do, just give me a holler. My cell number is right there on the bottom—it's always on."

He sets a heavy hand on Harriet's back and looks down on her with a meaningful gaze.

"Seriously," he says. "Give me a call. I mean it. I worry."

May 1, 1986
(HARRIET AT FORTY-NINE)

Yes, yes, we're all over the place again, pinballing across the decades, slinging and bumping our way through the days of your life, seemingly at random. And yes, pinball has come a long way since the Spot Bowler of your adolescence. They've added obstacles, pitfalls, bells, whistles, you name it. But look a little closer, Harriet, and you'll see there's a method to the madness, a logic to the game.

Of course, Caroline is on your mind, as you board the ferry in Kingston. Let's face it, for the ten-thousandth time, it was a mess from the beginning with Caroline, from before the beginning, in fact. God knows we won't start there. That's another place you refuse to revisit. But sooner or later, Harriet, you're gonna have to.

In the meantime, let's start in 1986.

Look at you, Harriet, in your shoulder pads and billowy sleeves, pushing the big five-oh! Once again, a little fuller of figure, a little longer of tooth. But your hair is, shall we say, very much of the times. Maybe a little young for a lady of your station, though in all fairness, that's only fitting for a woman who has just reclaimed her independence. That's right, your children are out of the house! What's on your flight itinerary, Harriet Chance, now that you've finally got that empty nest? Travel? A new hobby? A second shot at a career? What will you do with all those empty rooms? All that extra time?

Not so fast, Harriet.

Ground control, we've got a problem: Caroline has failed to launch. And let's be honest, that's a bit of an understatement. Not only is your daughter back from college, she won't leave the nest. As a matter of fact, she won't even leave her bedroom. She hardly eats, won't bathe, and doesn't return phone calls. She won't respond to your muffled inquiries, beyond three syllables. Softly, you hear the drone of the television, the monotonous pulse of rock music from behind her door. Other than that, not a sound.

Why don't you walk through that door, Harriet? What's stopping you, what are you afraid of?

Only late at night does Caroline leave her den, stealing wraithlike to the kitchen, or down the hall to the bathroom. You can hear her down there, so why do you lie in bed listening? Why don't you put on your slippers and bathrobe, walk down the stairs, and confront her?

The isolation lasts through early spring. And you let it, Harriet. Because, like a ball bearing, your path is smoother without friction. Because as much as you love your daughter, as deeply as you're attached to her, you cannot (or will not) resolve yourself to certain circumstances precipitating her very existence.

So, what's Bernard's excuse? Surely, from behind that crossword he sees his daughter withdrawing, just as sure as the heart of an adolescent woman is totally incomprehensible to him. And then there's this: if he starts looking too close, he may recognize something he doesn't want to see. What's a nine-letter word for turning a blind eye?

Finally, one fine morning, May Day, as it happens, you find Caroline's bedroom door wide open. Tentatively, you poke your head in, smiling as though the universe is in perfect balance, though there's pure dread in your heart. The bed is made. The drawers are empty. The record player is gone.

Yes, Harriet, you were worried sick. But admit it—c'mon, I dare you—you were the tiniest bit relieved.

You will not hear from your daughter for the next four months, until she calls you collect from a motel room in Albuquerque, New Mexico.

"Mom," she will say. "I need help."

August 19, 2015
(HARRIET AT SEVENTY-EIGHT)

When Harriet disembarks in Edmonds, Caroline's already waiting at the terminal, stationed like a crossing guard at the head of the gangway, head bobbing above the oncoming stream of commuters. Though Harriet stands a head shorter than anybody else, it would be hard to miss her—a slow eddy in a fast stream as she totters down the ramp, dragging her wheelie bag behind her. Spotting Harriet, Caroline begins waving both hands emphatically and working her way upstream, where she relieves Harriet of the suitcase.

"I'm parked up the hill," she says. "Do you want to wait here, and I'll go fetch the car?"

"No, no. I'll be fine."

"Where's Mildred?"

Silence, as Harriet looks down at the back of her hands.

"Where is she, Mom? Does she need help?"

"She's not coming."

Caroline stiffens. "What? What do you mean?"

"She canceled."

"Whoa, wait a minute, Mom. Not coming? What's wrong with her? Why didn't you tell me? Does Skip know?"

Harriet averts her eyes. "He wouldn't have let me come."

"You're right." She fishes her phone out of her purse. "I'm calling Skip."

Harriet takes hold of her wrist and looks meaningfully into her daughter's eyes. "Caroline, please."

Caroline looks curiously back at her for a long moment.

"Let me do this, dear," says Harriet.

Caroline runs a hand through her scraggly hair and sighs. "Fine. But Skip's not gonna be happy."

Within a half block, Harriet regrets the decision to walk. Even with Caroline pulling the bag, the incline presents a struggle. It takes them ten minutes to traverse the hill, and Harriet's exhausted long before they get to Caroline's dented Mazda.

"You all right, Mom?"

"Yes, dear," she says breathlessly.

By the time Harriet lowers herself into the passenger's seat, she's decidedly not fine. She's having a hot flash, as a matter of fact. Her breathing is ragged. Her scalp tingles. Goose flesh is rising on her forearms.

"You sure you're okay?"

"Just a bit winded, dear."

Reclining her head as much as her ailing neck will allow, Harriet closes her eyes and draws a few slow breaths as Caroline pulls away from the curb.

"Sorry again about the hill," Caroline says, reaching for the rear of the car. "I couldn't get any closer."

"That's fine, dear. The exercise was good."

Caroline plucks something off the backseat, and plops it in Harriet's lap. "I put together a few things for your trip."

"How thoughtful of you."

"Aren't you going to look?"

"Just resting my eyes, dear."

"A few creature comforts, that's all. I know it's not much. Just little things I always find myself wishing I had when I'm traveling."

Dutifully, Harriet opens her eyes, peering down into the pink gift bag for a quick inventory: a book of crossword puzzles, a roll of Tums, some orange foam ear plugs, and a pair of reading glasses.

"I hope those are strong enough," says Caroline. "The glasses, I mean."

"Oh yes, dear," Harriet says, closing her eyes once more. "They'll be perfect."

She can hardly get the last three words out, her tongue is so heavy. Within seconds, her thoughts lose all fluidity, hardening like wax in her brain, until her mind is a complete blank and her eyelids refuse to stay open. Soon Harriet is deeply and dreamlessly asleep in the passenger's seat.

When she awakens, much refreshed, somewhere around Everett, Caroline is sipping a latte, with the radio on low.

"There's a decaf latte there for you in the holder," she says. "Geez, Mom, I had no idea you could snore like that."

"I don't snore."

"Of course you don't."

"Well, you don't have to be rude about it," says Harriet, looking out the side window.

"Rude? I was—you were—ugh, never mind. Enjoy your latte."

Why does it always come to this between her and Caroline? As though they're out of patience before they've even begun. It doesn't seem to matter how firmly they resolve themselves to diplomacy or civil obligation, after the briefest of exchanges their relationship devolves into this prickly state of nervous exhaustion. They're forever plagued by the same old pettiness, still stung by the same insults, still harboring the same old resentments. Harriet knows damn well things might have gone better. She knows she should cut her daughter some slack, a lot of slack. But somehow she can't. And it pains her to admit that, if anything, Harriet has become less expansive with age. The fruits of self-pity were no less bitter at seventy-eight than they were at sixteen.

"You never give me enough credit," says Caroline. "You never have."

"Why, Caroline, darling, that's not true."

"It doesn't matter what I do, what I say, it's never enough. I'll always be a fucking addict to you."

"Oh, Caroline, stop, please. This has nothing to do with you. I'm an old woman, I've got a long day ahead of me. Thank you for picking me up. Thank you for the lovely gift bag. Thank you for the latte. I appreciate everything you do, truly, I do, but my goodness, Caroline, am I supposed to fall all over myself every time you carry a bag or buy me a cup of coffee? And must you always use such language?"

Caroline stares straight ahead at the road, stonily silent.

They maintain the silence past Mount Vernon, through tulip fields and the sprawl of light industrial, with the north Cascades rearing up out of the farmlands to the east. Harriet tries to nap again, but sleep won't have her.

"I'm sorry, dear," she says, at last. "Forgive me, I was exhausted from the walk."

"I told you, I'd get the car."

"I didn't mean it that way. And I'm sorry you feel I never gave you enough credit. Oh, Caroline, I've failed in so many ways, I know that."

"You favored Skip."

The observation is so unexpected, so out of context, that Harriet finds it momentarily disorienting. "Why, Caroline, that's not true. Dear, how can you even say that?"

"Because it was obvious."

"In what way?"

"It was like we were competing."

"Competing? Caroline, I would never pit my children in competition. What kind of mother do you think I was?"

"No, you and I."

Harriet is dumbstruck.

"You treated me like a rival, Mom."

Stunned by the realization, Harriet stares numbly at the wrinkled hands piled in her lap.

"Was it any wonder I hated Skip growing up? He got everything, all of Dad's attention. You and I had to split what was left while Skip got to *do* everything. And I was expected to stand on the sidelines like you, like a cheerleader, rooting for Skip. So Skip could go to camp, so Skip could get a scholarship, so Skip could—"

"You went to camp, dear."

"You made me," she says. She sets her coffee in the holder next to Harriet's untouched latte and grips the wheel fiercely with both hands. "Skip was the one who wanted to go. I hated it."

"Good grief, Caroline, that was 1976!"

"You were cheap with me—just like you were cheap with yourself."

"It's hardly as if we were wealthy."

"Cheap in other ways. Oh, forget it," she says, waving it off. "I should have eaten something."

"Well, goodness," says Harriet, reaching into her gift bag. "Let's stop and eat, then. I have until four o'clock to board. It'll do us both good."

Peeling back the foil wrapper of her Tums, Harriet pops one in her mouth, replacing the roll in the pink bag as the antacid begins its chalky dissolve, coating the inside of her mouth.

She doubts whether she can actually eat, but the change of scenery and the presence of other people can't hurt. Fishing her compact out of her purse, she refreshes her lipstick.

At a Denny's just off the interstate south of Bellingham, they sit in a booth across the aisle from the window. Caroline orders a club sandwich and bowl of minestrone. Harriet orders the avocado chicken Caesar, without avocados. They maintain silence as they wait for their food, Caroline checking her cell phone distractedly. She looks haggard and worry-worn, her eyes rimmed blue-black. Harriet can see that her nails are bitten to the quick.

"You look tired, dear."

"Gee, thanks, Mom."

"I didn't mean it that way. I'm just concerned. How *are* you? How is Cassidy? Have you heard from her?"

"What do you think?"

"Have you seen the baby yet?"

"No."

"Are you talking?"

And that's when Caroline does a most unexpected thing: she casts her eyes down, clutches her face in her hands, and begins sobbing.

Harriet reaches both hands across the table.

"Goodness, dear, I'm so sorry. Is everything okay? Did something happen with Cassidy's baby?"

Caroline wipes her eyes, blurring her mascara, then extends a hand, which Harriet sandwiches between her own.

"Dear, what is it? What's wrong?"

Caroline withdraws her hand gently and straightens up.

"Oh, Mom, it's nothing, okay? I just made a mess of my life."

Studying her from across the table, Harriet can still see beyond the worried lines of her daughter's drawn face, beyond the graying hair and the drooping flesh of middle age, past the two failed marriages, the drugs and alcohol, the numerous career changes, the countless disappointments and indignities, to the roly-poly toddler, the gap-toothed little girl, and the sullen teenager with whom she'd fought so bitterly. Though Caroline has achieved varying degrees of success, known fleeting triumphs and sporadic fulfillment, she has not lived a happy life. And somehow, Harriet suddenly sees herself responsible for all of it, every dashed hope, every shade of disillusionment.

"That settles it," she says. "We're turning around. We're going directly to your house, and I'm staying the week. Longer, if necessary."

"No, Mom, slow down, really. I'm fine."

"Please, Caroline, dear, let me do something. Let me come stay for a week. I'm more useful than I look. I can cook and clean and run errands. I can—"

"Mom, really, no. I was just having a moment, okay?"

"It's the change of life, isn't it, dear?"

"No, it isn't, Mom. I wish it were that simple. Sometimes I

just start thinking about my life, you know, the parts I can't have back. But it's good, reflection is good. I'm fine."

"You're sure?"

"I'm positive."

With that, Caroline flags the waitress, and in spite of Harriet's protestations, insists on picking up the tab—tipping nearly thirty percent!

"Dear, check your math," says Harriet, dutifully. "Fifteen percent of twenty-seven is roughly four dollars."

"Hello, Mom, get with the program. Fifteen percent was decades ago. These days, it's eighteen percent minimum—and that's just for cheapskates and large parties. These people don't have benefits. They have no job security. It's cruel to tip less than twenty-five percent."

Harriet's determined not to haggle, though fifteen percent has always seemed fair. Besides, she's proud of Caroline. Generosity, after all, is one of the few virtues that trumps thrift.

"Whatever you say, dear."

They leave their food half eaten and drive mostly in silence through Ferndale, toward the border crossing at Blaine. Caroline loosens her grip on the wheel and rolls her shoulders several times to ease the tension.

"I'm glad I broke down back there," she says. "It was a relief. I needed to get it out."

"I'm glad, dear."

Harriet reaches over and rests a hand on Caroline's thigh and gives it a few loving pats. A dense, almost unbearable grief wells in Harriet's chest as she withdraws her hand. Harriet, too, is thinking of a life she can't have back. Tentatively, she replaces her hand on Caroline's lap.

"Dear?" she says. "I know where you stand on the church, but . . . would it be okay if I . . ."

"Sure," she says, producing a sad smile. "You can pray for me. That would be fine."

December 19, 1953
(HARRIET AT SEVENTEEN)

 flipper here, a bumper there, a kicker, a spinner, a roll-over, and ding-dong-ding, we're in the waning days of 1953.

Who is that striking young lady just left of the mistletoe, poised in the sapphire blue evening dress with the portrait collar, looking ladylike in her long white gloves—the one who looks like a slightly chubby Susan Hayward? Well, in the right light, anyway, at the right angle, after enough buttered rum. Why, it's you, Harriet Nathan, at your father's Christmas party. Teddy Ballgame is six months back from Korea (along with your future husband). They've got a chimp on television now. They say this H-bomb makes Little Boy look like a party favor. And it's not just bombs—everything is getting bigger and louder.

Look at you, Harriet, hair expertly coiffed, hobnobbing with the partners like you were born to it. So composed, so effortlessly buoyant, as you play the part of a woman. At forty, you'll wonder what became of all that finesse, all that poise. But for now, your father is grooming you. If he has his way, you'll be a credit to your sex. Weekdays, you'll trade evening dresses for a woman's business attire. You'll make a name for yourself. Or better yet, you'll stick with the name you were given. The click of your heels down courthouse corridors will one day strike fear in the hearts of opposing counsel.

Your father's ambition is contagious, and maybe not beyond your reach. Next year, you'll graduate high school and pursue that law degree he's picked out for you. From there, with enough elbow grease, a formidable network, and a little luck, it's up up up, Ms. Nathan. The world is your oyster.

But let us not forget, you're only a girl, Harriet. Only seven weeks removed from your seventeenth birthday. You still dream of horses, still slurp malted milks and play pinball down at Sully's. You've only been past first base a few times, and God knows, they didn't really count (how could they!). You're still not sure what you want for yourself or to which pressures you might succumb. Yes, Harriet, behind that feminine mystique is a girl who just got her drivers' license last summer.

Maybe Charlie Fitzsimmons didn't get the memo. Maybe he ignored it. Wouldn't be the first time. Charlie has a way of getting around rules. The man can smell a loophole ten miles away. Yes, the whiz kid is fast becoming Old Charlie. After twenty years at the firm, he's practically family. Like a trusted uncle, or an uncle, anyway. It's complicated. Charlie confides in you, always has, ever since you were a kid.

Tonight is no exception. In the half-darkened hallway, where you've just emerged from straightening your hair in the washroom, and you've barely replaced your white gloves, Charlie all but corners you. Desperate for somebody's confidence, he tells you—you, of all people, Harriet Nathan—of his plans to leave the firm and start his own shop. They keep adding names to the marble slab, but Nathan will always be first. Charlie wants his own shingle. Yes, Charlie's ambitious, too. He gets what he wants. And he never forgets a friend. He'll have a job waiting for you, he promises, but you mustn't tell your father of his plans. Deal?

Smell his cologne, smell the rum on his breath, as he crowds in so close you can't tell where one smell ends and the other begins. All but pinning you to the wall, he whispers. What surprises you about his groping hands is their boyish clumsiness.

In six months, Charlie Fitzsimmons will make good on his plans and leave the firm, opening his own shop less than two blocks away. Though there's a few hard feelings with the Nathans, Charlie will remain a presence in your life, dropping you a line now and then as you pursue your degree, and each time he'll remind you of that job that's waiting for you.

You'll never breathe a word of it to your father.

August 19, 2015
(HARRIET AT SEVENTY-EIGHT)

When Caroline pulls into Departures, easing to a stop curbside behind a long line of yellow cabs, the reception area is swarming with humanity.

"They probably won't let me go all the way, Mom. But let me at least park and help you as far as check-in."

"No, dear. I'll be perfectly fine."

"You're sure?"

"Yes, of course."

As they say their good-byes, Caroline eases back into traffic. Harriet stands in place, watching as the Mazda rounds the corner. As usual, she feels as though she's missed an opportunity.

A voice from behind startles her. Harriet turns to find

herself facing an unfortunate young man with acne-scarred cheeks.

"May I check your bags?" he says.

"Oh, no," Harriet says, gripping her wheelie bag tighter. "Thank you, dear, I'm keeping my bags with me."

She's heard too many horror stories about mischecked and mismanaged luggage. Why, Barbara Chatsworth's trip to Omaha had been virtually ruined last Christmas when her bags ended up in Wichita. The poor dear had to wear her son's old Mackinaw jacket to *The Nutcracker*. And if that weren't enough, she couldn't curl her hair for a week.

"But ma'am, if you let me check it, the baggage will be waiting for you in your cabin," he says, reaching for the wheelie bag.

"No thank you, dear."

"Suit yourself," he says, with a shrug. "But you'll have to roll the bag through customs and the rest of it. It's a hassle." He looks down at her, doubtfully. "And it's hot in there, ma'am."

Though the young man is making good sense, Harriet can't stop thinking about Barbara Chatsworth in that baggy Mackinaw, her hair hanging in straggles. How dull the Dance of the Sugar Plum Fairy must have sounded to poor Barbara that evening.

"All the same, I'll just keep the bag with me. Now, could you kindly direct me to my vessel, dear?"

He waves vaguely down the corridor. "Just follow the signs."

Hobbling into the fray, Harriet finds herself immediately disoriented by all the activity. The bright corridor is crammed wall-to-wall with people, every last one of them moving more purposefully than Harriet. Within thirty feet, she regrets not having checked the bag. By the time she reaches the dogleg, where the corridor empties into a giant terminal, the mass of people spreading out like liquid, Harriet is out of breath.

There are signs, all right. Too many. Some of them in foreign languages. There are arrows, hallways, monitors, glass doors, and kiosks—all of them beginning to look a little fuzzy around the edges. Weak in the knees, Harriet spins a slow half circle, scanning the terminal, looking desperately for a uniform—any uniform. But the longer Harriet searches, the closer her uneasiness noses toward anxiety.

Finally, like an angel, she appears: a smooth-faced Asian woman, whose age Harriet puts somewhere between thirteen and forty-five. An almond-eyed beauty, with no makeup and no wedding ring. She sets the daintiest of hands on Harriet's back.

"You are lost?" she says.

"Yes, dear, I'm afraid I am."

"Do you have boarding pass?"

Harriet digs her plastic pouch out of her purse and begins rummaging through it.

"May I?" the woman gently urges.

"Please," says Harriet, handing over the pouch.

The woman flips through the papers efficiently until she locates the boarding pass, which she surveys expertly.

"Ah," she says. "Follow me."

"You're a lifesaver, dear."

"Call me Sinta."

Not only does dear Sinta escort Harriet through the labyrinthine confusion of the central terminal to customs, all the while maintaining a manageable pace, she is kind enough to convey the wheelie bag for the duration of the journey. Sinta even offers to assist Harriet with her declaration forms.

"Oh, no, I'll be fine, thank you," she hears herself saying.

The twenty minutes it takes to fill out her declaration forms proves restful. Nerves settled, Harriet joins the customs line, which switches back and forth at least twenty times on its way across a giant receiving room. Line is a misnomer—it's a throng, a veritable stockyard. The young man with the pitted cheeks had not been exaggerating the conditions: it's hot in there, all right. Stifling. The air is oppressive, the odors too various to catalog—butter, sweat, the unmistakable boiled-egg offal of flatulence. And Harriet is certain she's identified the culprit on the latter count: the morbidly obese fellow in a sleeveless T-shirt, the one with the dirty baseball cap that says DAMN STRAIGHT! A gentleman might have had the decency to step out of line and find a bathroom. At the very least, he might apologize. And certainly his shirt would have sleeves.

The longer Harriet lingers in the interminable line, creeping forward by the tiniest of increments, the lower her opinion of humanity sinks. Gads, but look at us. Like cattle. Sweating, stinking, overfed cattle. Surely, the species is devolving, even as culture accelerates, speeding headlong at an unstoppable pace toward what was sure to be a brick wall. Values erode, as waistlines bulge, timeworn conventions like polite deference to elders and good citizenry go the way of the powdered wig. And eventually, sleeves disappear.

Oh, Harriet knows she's simply exhausted, she knows if she could ever manage to locate her cabin and get off her feet for a few minutes, her attitude would improve. Finally, after forty-five minutes of glacial progress, Harriet reaches the front of the line and at some length proffers her passport and forms as the customs agent, his reading glasses roosting on the bridge of his nose, peers benignly down at her from his podium, subjecting the passport to a cursory once-over before passing it back.

"Not packing any fruits or vegetables?"

"No."

"Not carrying in excess of ten thousand dollars in Canadian currency?"

"Heavens, no. Will I be needing Canadian currency on board?"

"No ma'am. Are you transporting anything on behalf of a second party, or were you approached or otherwise solicited to transport goods on anyone else's behalf?"

"Pardon me? I don't understand. Do you mean Sinta?"

The customs agent says something quietly over his shoulder to a security officer. The next thing Harriet knows, a second agent is at her elbow, asking her to step aside, even as the officer steps forward, taking possession of her wheelie bag.

"Is there some problem?" Harriet inquires.

But neither the officer or the second agent are willing to offer her an explanation. "This way, please," says the agent.

Bewildered, Harriet is escorted down a hallway to a nearby holding room, one of several small, less-than-cheery rooms on either side of the corridor.

"Sit, please," says the officer as the second agent leaves the room. Harriet's heart is racing as she lowers herself into a metal folding chair.

The officer, a younger man than either of the agents, with muscular arms and a slight underbite, pulls up a second folding chair and seats himself directly across from Harriet, whereupon he silently considers her for what feels like an eternity.

"Who is Sinta?"

"You mean the young lady who assisted me with my bag?"

He frowns. "Do you know Sinta? What's her last name?"

"I have no idea. I assumed she worked here."

"She approached you? Where? In the terminal?"

"Yes. She could see I was quite lost. I might have fallen to the floor and had a heart attack in there, and people would have stepped right over me. Sinta was the only one kind enough to help me with my bag."

"So, she touched the bag?"

"She rolled the blasted thing clear across the terminal. If it weren't for the dear woman, I might never have arrived here."

"I see. Did she ask you to transport anything for her?"

"I don't understand."

"Did she open your bag or your purse? Did she offer you anything?"

"Why, she only helped me with my papers."

The officer looks down at her grimly. "What papers? She touched them?"

Even as he drills her, Harriet can see two dark-haired men through the glass, rummaging through her wheelie bag. All that meticulous packing, all that tucking and folding and consolidating for nothing.

"What is the meaning of this? Just what are you alluding to with all of these questions? And why are those men making a shambles of my toiletries?"

No sooner does Harriet lodge this complaint than she sees one of the dark-haired officials unearth the Greek yogurt container from the bottom of her suitcase. Subjecting the parcel to a wary visual inspection, he soon hands it off to the other man, who proceeds to shake the receptacle a number of times like a maraca. Much to Harriet's discomfiture, he promptly removes the seal, peels back the lid, and peers down into the depths, which both men regard with suspicion, alternately sniffing and discussing the contents before the taller of the two men, a reedy fellow with dark circles beneath his eyes, inexplicably dips a tentative finger into Bernard's remains and touches it to his tongue.

Harriet shoots up from her chair. "Good heavens, what are they doing?"

But before she can protest further, she watches through the glass as a rather skittish Doberman pinscher is escorted into the room and persuaded to sniff Bernard's mortal remains.

"What on earth? I've never heard of such a thing. Do I look like a terrorist to you? For heaven's sake, I'm Episcopalian!"

Before Harriet can finish dressing down the officer, the man with the dark circles pokes his head in.

"She's clean," he says.

The officer frowns. Resting his hands on his knees, he pushes himself out of his chair. "We're sorry about the inconvenience, ma'am."

Across the hall, Harriet is forced to produce her passport again and sign for her bags. She's led down the hallway and delivered to an empty podium at the head of another receiving area, where instantly she's relieved to spot a sign that says MS ZUIDERDAM. She can't help but beam her approval at the young woman who greets her at the podium.

"May I see your boarding pass and your declaration form, please?"

Harriet nimbly produces the items from her pouch and passes them to the young woman, who inspects them both smilingly before passing them back.

"Perfect," she says, turning her attention to her computer, where her fingers begin tap-dancing on the keyboard. "Hmm," she says, after a lot of tapping. "It says here we don't have your questionnaire."

"Excuse me?"

"You were supposed to fill out a hospitality questionnaire online."

"Dear, but I—"

"How did you book your reservation?"

"By telephone, of course."

"So you never received the questionnaire?"

"No."

The woman frowns. "Wait here."

She confers in low tones with a bearded associate as a line begins to stack up behind Harriet. When the woman returns, she's clutching a packet. Harriet's heart sinks.

"Ma'am, can I ask you to step aside here? Just have a seat at that table, and someone will be right with you."

She corrals Harriet briskly to a nearby fold-out table, where she pulls out a chair.

"Go ahead and fill this out," she says, producing a pen from behind her ear.

Harriet looks dully down at the packet, weary beyond outrage. Mechanically, she picks up the pen and begins filling out the questionnaire.

Ten minutes after completing the packet, nobody has come for her. Her patience, already frayed at the edges, begins to unravel. She's ready to stand up and begin yelling, ready to take somebody to task. My God, her hands are shaking by the time another young woman arrives to collect her packet. Harriet scarcely has time to begin complaining before she's promptly presented to yet another agent and asked to surrender her boarding pass again. The young man scans the paper with a red light, producing a beep, then smiles.

"Enjoy your cruise," he says. "Watch your step."

And just like that, the ordeal is over. Harriet passes through a sliding glass door and begins inching her way up the pier toward the gangway.

November 19, 2014
(HARRIET AT SEVENTY-EIGHT)

old on tight, Harriet, we're off and racing again, careening past switches, gates, and stoppers, ding-ding-ding, thwack off a live kicker, and currently hurtling headlong toward the drain. Yep, everything moves quicker now, everything but your reactions.

Welcome to your not-so-distant past, Harriet Chance. Look at you, dressed in black, all the way down to your orthopedic shoes. Today you bury your husband of fifty-five years. Well, not exactly bury. Hey, it wasn't an easy decision, but it had to be made. No use in debating it now.

Wanting to avoid a big ceremony, you see to the arrangements with minimal fanfare. A sleepy wake at the Carlsborg house. Just Skip and Caroline, Mildred, and Father Mullinix.

Caroline is biting her nails, and Skip is rummaging through the refrigerator as Mildred busies herself around your kitchen. Ever the helper, your friend sets out a cheese plate, some cranberry scones, makes a pot of her signature weak coffee. Thank God for Mildred. And thank God for Father Mullinix, a stationary presence on the sofa, nibbling, and looking strong.

Some pleasant conversation, tempered by grief, a few tears, and some nervous laughter ensue. You handle yourself courageously, Harriet.

In the backyard, Father Mullinix, brushing crumbs from his gown, deems cremation an acceptable form of Christian burial, then proceeds to share a few words on the subject of immortal souls, along with a little hope and assurance from the book of Job. A little Corinthians for good measure. And a welcome moment of levity when he nearly drops the urn.

Finally, flanked by your middle-aged children, with your loyal friend Mildred clutching your hand, a scattering of ashes and a smattering of bone chips beneath the bare lilac as some but not all of your husband's mortal remains are returned to the earth. Somehow you could only scatter half of him.

All in all, a nice send-off, if not a little subdued, for the man you spent the majority of your life with. Yes, Harriet, you preferred to grieve quietly rather than demonstratively. Yes, you preferred a small, sober gathering of family to the spectacle of an open casket, and a receiving line of once-familiar faces and misplaced names. My God, you haven't seen the Blums in twenty-five years, why would you want to grieve with them?

But grieving aside, Harriet, let's talk about the real reason you had Bernard reduced to ashes and not buried beneath a maple in accordance with his wishes (for heaven's sake, he bought the plot twenty-five years ago). Admit it, the real reason you chose cremation was because you yearned to see his mortal shell pulverized. You hated his body for betraying him—for betraying both of you. He was a walking, talking corpse those last eighteen months. His brain began decomposing long before his breathing stopped. His bowels and bladder were not far behind. Oh, he was strong, right up to the end, though, wasn't he? He could overpower you with his infantile rage, and did on numerous occasions, resulting in bumps, scrapes, bruises, even one black eye, which you attributed to the car door.

C'mon, admit it, Harriet, irrational as it may be, to a large degree, you hold him responsible for those last terrible years—including your own failure, Sherwood Arms, the fall, every last sordid detail. Still, those years give off such a glare that you can't bear to look at them. Not today, not next week, but sometime soon, Harriet, you're gonna have to.

August 19, 2015
(HARRIET AT SEVENTY-EIGHT)

Some seven hours after Dwight picked her up at her doorstep, Harriet, nerve-worn, famished, and aching, finally sets foot on the carpeted promenade of the *Zuiderdam*, with a silent prayer of thanks on her lips. The worst is over—it has to be—and Harriet has survived mostly intact. Her relief, while considerable, is short-lived, as the line of boarding cruisers empties into a chaotic scrum on the mezzanine, where the bulk of the mob elbows for position before the elevator bank, while a few courageous cruisers with the strength and wherewithal brave the wide carpeted stairway to the upper promenade.

She gropes around in her purse, withdraws her reading glasses, and scans her itinerary for her cabin assignment until the mezzanine is all but empty.

"Here, let me take a peek at that," says a voice from behind.

Harriet turns to discover none other than the flatulent young giant in the sleeveless T-shirt from the customs line.

"C'mon," he says after a cursory scan of her boarding pass. "Y'all are on Rotterdam, just a couple doors down from me."

His breathing is labored from exertion. There's a little rattle in his throat. Lumbering across the mezzanine, he parks both wheelie bags in front of the elevator bank, pushes the call button, and mops the sweat from his forehead with a hairy forearm.

"Kurt Pickens," he says, extending a hand.

"Harriet Chance."

"No kiddin'? Went to school with a fella named Boyd Chance. You got people in Bath County?"

"Not to my knowledge, dear."

"Where y'all from?"

"Washington State, dear."

"How about that? Owingsville, Kentucky, here. This is us," he announces as the elevator door opens on a long stretch of ghastly carpet.

Dragging the luggage, Kurt guides her down a cramped hallway toward the rear of the vessel. He's sweating again after thirty feet.

"Whoooeee," he says, catching his breath. "They don't make it no cake walk now, do they?"

"No, they certainly don't."

At last, Kurt deposits her in front of her cabin door, where he instructs her on the use of her card key, his great midsection still heaving.

"Bless you, Mr. Pickens."

"Y'all have a good cruise now," he says, resuming his ungainly stride. "See you at the buffet."

The cabin, furnished roughly as it had been in the brochure, is half the size it appeared in the photos. The decor is bland and inoffensive: beiges and muted pastels, rattan and smoked glass. The art, nautically themed, is inconspicuous. The overall effect is an airport Radisson in miniature.

Harriet immediately unzips her wheelie bag and checks on Bernard's ashes. Finding the container intact, she sets it atop the dresser, then lowers herself into the love seat, hoping against hope that she'll be able to lift herself out again.

If things keep up at this pace, she'll drop dead before Skagway, a thought that—at the moment—is less disconcerting than it should be. Closing her eyes, she takes several deep breaths and stares at the back of her eyelids.

Dear Lord, forgive me for questioning your wisdom. I've leaned on my own understanding, and I've had moments of doubt. But I have not lost faith, Lord.

She feels better immediately. It's all out of her hands now. Before long, her body is one with the quilted cushion of the love seat as the heavy veil of sleep descends.

Then sunlight floods the room.

Harriet turns sleepily to meet a gentle breeze, and there, standing on the veranda not ten feet from her, clad in a crisp gray coverall, hair Brylcreemed to a shine, stands Bernard, looking just as he did when she first met him in 1957.

"Lot of hand sanitizer," he observes. "That's good. You get a GI breakout on this tub, and bingo bango, there goes your cruise. They've got dispensers at the end of every hallway—every twenty feet on the Lido deck. Not the most decorative things, soap dispensers, but smart."

"Oh, Bernard, you're coming."

"You tell me," he says, crossing the threshold, whereupon he begins subjecting the room to a casual inspection—squeezing throw pillows, opening cabinets, running his fingers over the desktop, then checking them for dust.

"Kind of small," he concludes. "But efficient. How's the water pressure?"

"I haven't tested it."

"Meals included?"

"Yes, buffet and dining room."

Jutting his lower lip out, he nods, mildly impressed, as he raps a wall with his knuckles to determine its thickness, then pauses to inspect the framed print above the love seat, tilting his head curiously one way, then back the other.

He's so close, Harriet can smell him, his Brylcreem, his starch, and yes, even his hand sanitizer.

"I feel so strange," says Harriet. "Am I . . . dead?"

"Not yet," he says, examining the television remote. "Trust me, you'll know."

"Should I be frightened?"

"Won't do you any good," he says, setting the remote aside. "Don't bother planning."

"That doesn't sound like you. You made our burial arrangements the day we moved to the peninsula."

"Twelve ninety-nine was a steal. Copper deluxe caskets, hardwood—the good stuff."

Here he drifts absently toward the bedroom portion of the cabin, pausing at the dresser to pick up the yogurt container, considering its weight before reading the label.

"Good plot, right? Conveniently located. Shady, not too crowded. Nice place to be buried."

"It's beautiful, I'm sorry. I know you would have preferred it that way. I was just . . . it was selfish of me."

He waves it off. "Look, I understand. Who needs all the ceremony at a time like that. And what's the difference? I take up less space this way. And think of the money you'll save on flowers."

Gently, he sets down the ashes. "Glacier Bay, huh? Not what I had in mind for a final resting place exactly."

"You don't approve?"

"Actually, I'm starting to like the idea. Look, there's something I've gotta tell you. You deserve to know. Things we can't plan for—they happen, Harriet."

"You think I don't know that?"

"I'm not talking about Alzheimer's. I'm talking about . . . situations. Not ideal ones. We cause them to happen even when we don't mean to. We're weak, Harriet, and I was weaker than most. The best we can hope for is forgiveness. I hope you can accept that."

"It sounds like an apology."

"It is." He turns to face her directly. "But it probably won't do me any good."

Slowly, still facing her, he backs between the parted drapes and onto the veranda. "I really am sorry," he says, receding.

"You shouldn't be," she says, a sleepy smile clinging to her face.

April 16, 1973
(HARRIET AT THIRTY-SIX)

It's true, Harriet, there are a few cracks beginning to show in the foundation of your marriage by the time you reach your ivory anniversary. But that's a normal part of the continuum. Having apparently said all that needed to be said over the years, you and Bernard don't talk much anymore. You haven't had sexual relations in months. How long since you played a game of Scrabble or went to a movie? Again, nothing catastrophic, nothing that's going to bring down the house, just the ruinous effects of time and familiarity.

Love grows quieter, Harriet, it's true. People evolve, or they don't. Either way, they grow apart. Sometimes they get busy. It's not as if ball bearings are threatening to kill your family life, but last week Bernard missed Caroline's birthday and

Skip's home opener. Tonight he will miss the occasion of your anniversary. But to his credit, he will remember the day and phone you from his hotel room, summoning the appropriate enthusiasm. And you'll be glad to hear his voice.

Yes, all in all, things could be a lot worse. You could be divorced. You could be a widow. Gallo could stop selling wine by the jug. And where would that leave you, Harriet? Bored *and* sober.

The fact is, you've adjusted your expectations. You're no longer a romantic. After fourteen years of marriage and two children, the glass slipper no longer fits. But being Mrs. Bernard Chance isn't so bad. If not happy, you're comfortable. You have two bright, healthy children and a nice house in a desirable neighborhood. Your refrigerator is always full, and every year so are those Christmas stockings. And though you're relations have tapered off, and boredom has set in, seventeen years after he showed up at Fourth and Union clutching a bouquet, Bernard, still handsome, though frequently absent, perpetually grumpy, and often elusive, is still your husband, still the man you aim to spend the rest of your days with.

And you wouldn't have it any other way.

This is your life, Harriet, for better or worse, in sickness and in health, until death do you part.

August 19, 2015
(HARRIET AT SEVENTY-EIGHT)

The dreamy smile still clings to Harriet's face, as she pushes herself out of the love seat and begins unpacking her suitcase. Refolding her clothing (good heavens, those animals at customs have made a mess of it), she nestles each garment neatly into its tiny drawer, now and again smiling her satisfaction at Bernard's ashes, atop the dresser. It's as if he's still in the room. She swears she can still smell his Brylcreem.

All settled in, Harriet perches on the edge of the bed, reaching for her purse. Remembering Mildred's envelope, she debates whether she should even read it, at the risk of souring her mood. But she can't help herself. She tears the envelope open, and removes the thick letter, folded in three.

My Dearest Harriet,

I've been trying for months to tell you in person, but I just couldn't muster the courage. For years, I've been unworthy of your friendship and exploited your generosity. You've been the truest and most loyal friend I've ever had, and I've thanked you by withholding things for so long that my conscience simply can't take it any longer.

It feels like I'm running out of time, and there's so much I need to explain. But I feel that I must account for my actions before I can hope for the Lord's mercy and that I must seek your forgiveness before I may ask as much of the Almighty. Hopefully, at least one of you can see clear to forgive me, though I will understand perfectly if you are unable to. Darling, I do hope you are sitting down.

What I have to tell you will come as a shock, but you deserve to know. Clark, may he rest in peace, never had the benefit of knowing. But I now see that nothing is covered up that will not be revealed, or hidden that will not be known. I will not make the same mistake with you that I did with Clark. I can promise you will never look at me the same after I tell you what I must tell you.

In 1973, after twenty-two years of marriage to Clark, I met a man. What can I say but that this man was very different from Clark, and he took me completely by surprise. I was not unhappy in my marriage, not even dissatisfied. Clark was a good man, a good father, and a great provider, if not a little absent. Together, we brought Dwight into the world, we lived in a beautiful home in Edmonds, we had many friends. I had much to lose. But as I said, this affair took me totally by surprise.

Though this other man and I lived for years within ten miles of one another on the north end of Seattle, we met on the other side of the continent, in a coffee shop near the old Philadelphia Civic Center, where he was on business, and I was in Camden making arrangements for my mother's burial. It was only whim that brought me to the city that morning. I needed to get away from it all—my father, the arrangements, that old house, with all its memories. I suppose I was looking for nothing more than an escape. I will not burden you with the details of our first encounter, except to say that it was chance, but it did not feel that way.

I've often thought that were it not for my emotional state, I would not have taken up with this man, that if Clark would have been at my side during these dark hours, instead of in New York with pressing business, I would not have felt the need for such a companion. If my mother had died two days earlier, if Dwight had come from Bozeman with his new girl-friend, if I'd not taken a bus downtown, if I'd not happened upon this coffee shop and seen the pies in the window, had I not sat at the counter instead of a booth—if any one of these things had gone differently, I likely would not have met this man, and my life for the next four decades would have been very different.

But these are only excuses. Wishful thinking has taken me

as far as it can take me. Whatever the circumstances leading up to our meeting, no matter how coincidental or seemingly fated our association, I now take full responsibility for my actions. That it has taken me four decades to do so is disgraceful.

This man, it turned out, was also married, and happily so. He had two children, a king's set, boy and a girl, along with a loyal and supportive wife, of whom he always spoke highly. These things he told me before I knew his last name. So, you see, he, too, had everything to lose. How can I explain how we thought our association was worth risking everything but to say that the decision seemed inevitable? How can I explain my attraction to such a man but to say that it was contrary to any other attraction I had felt before? He was not as refined as Clark, not in his manners, or his tastes, or even in his emotional sophistication, but he was sincere and quietly strong in a way that Clark wasn't. And he was troubled, too, by the world, and by the ways of his own heart, and I suppose I thought I could save him. It's an old storyline that never ends well.

We met on two more occasions before he left Philadelphia for his family. He left on the Sunday I buried my mother, and I had no intention of ever seeing the man again; that is to say, I had every intention of never seeing him again, though I knew with every nerve in my body that I must. And this is how I felt about the man for the next thirty-odd years.

What must you think of me, now? Sneaking around all those years, abusing the confidence and generosity of a husband who provided for all but one of my needs—a need that had not existed until I met this other man at the age of forty?

How could I have been capable of such deceit? How could I live with myself, knowing that Clark had no clue as to my duplicity, nursed not even the slightest suspicion of my infidelity? That's how much he trusted me. All those years, off and on, I had extramarital relations with another man, and Clark carried on as usual, buying me bouquets and complimenting my weak coffee.

As Clark and I passed our golden years together, it seemed natural that our relations should tail off, that our love should mellow, at least in its physical expression. This was not the case with the other man. We still coupled like young newlyweds late into our sixties. Living as we did on stolen hours, our association was only physical in the sense that there seemed to be no more immediate solution to bridging the distance between us.

Understand that never in all these years did I confuse my love for Clark with my love for the other man. One, though practiced, and requiring at times no little effort, was calm and steady, while the other, effortless, reckless, ranged anywhere from tumultuous to chaotic. Never did I discuss or even consider leaving Clark for the other man, nor he his family.

In 1984, I tried to end the association. Clark, having retired the previous year, was for the first time in our thirty-four year marriage, not absent. On the contrary, he was very present. He hardly came or went at all. Logistically, the association became more difficult to maintain and, by extension, more secretive. Our meetings became less frequent, more harried, and for the first time, ambivalent. Suddenly, we spent less time coupling and more time scheming. These limitations to our freedom soon exacted their toll. The less time we spent together, the more we quarreled. For the first time, the association was beginning to exhibit all the trappings of an unhappy relationship. I began to see the man differently. Those very qualities I had once idealized, I now saw in a more unflattering light. And when I began to suggest we break off the association, new qualities emerged in my lover: Jealousy. Possessiveness. He became a tyrant with his opinions. He lowered my opinion of myself. And such was my guilt by then that I began to need this, too. It was as if by punishing myself, I could undo everything that came before. The less respect he paid me, the more I needed him to achieve balance. For here was the love I deserved, the love I had earned.

Clark never cared enough to suspect a thing. All those years, he was more interested in his *Wall Street Journal* than he was interested in me. But something happened when he retired. Suddenly he was present. Suddenly he was taking an interest in my ever-evolving worldview.

I felt certain the move to Sequim in '85 would end the association for good. The very day that Clark and I committed to the idea, I broke it off with the other man. Not face-to-face, not with a phone call, but like this, with a letter. I know I'm a coward. I gave him no forwarding address, no number, and only the vaguest references with regard to our relocation. It was a clean break. And God, but what a relief it was to let go, to put the thing behind me.

Sequim was the perfect opportunity for a second chance. I was ready to reinvent myself and erase my past. I was ravenous to be someone else completely. I was ready to respect myself so that I could respect others—specifically, Clark. At fifty-eight, I was ready to be the woman Clark deserved. I owed it to him. And by God, that first year in Sequim, I improved myself. I took classes at the community center. I became quite active at St. Luke's. I began to explore my inner self in ways that had formerly never occurred to me. Inch by inch, I was expanding. And the church was only the beginning of my spiritual inquiry. I discovered the public library. I dabbled and experimented in a variety of alternative health regimens and holistic philosophies. I stopped eating wheat, I practiced self-care and nurturance.

And Clark, dear Clark, finally a husband, he encouraged me every step and every leap of the way. We began to get acquainted as though for the first time, and it was thrilling. I felt like a new person, like I'd been given a fresh start. Clark proved himself capable of things I never even suspected. We went skydiving on our thirty-fifth anniversary, hand in hand.

Then, one Sunday morning everything changed. No sooner had I taken my seat beside Clark at St. Luke's than I saw him, the other man, and I knew in that instant that no faith or discipline could save me. Of all the churches in all the world, there he was, and I was doomed, just as sure as I was doomed when I walked into that coffee shop in Philadelphia thirteen years earlier. There he sat, directly across from me, third pew, just left of center, glasses halfway down the bridge of his nose, a crossword in his lap. And there beside him, attentive and right at home, was you.

Harriet swoons, the letter slipping from her grasp. Only dimly is she aware of the pages scattering as they flutter to the carpet. Her ears are ringing. Her legs are numb. The room spins slowly. Bracing herself on the edge of the bed, she feels her heart kicking at her rib cage, as though desperate to escape. She believes in this moment that she's dying.

August 18, 1965
(HARRIET AT TWENTY-EIGHT)

Uh, well, ummm, yeah. Hello? Hello? Nudge, nudge. We're frozen here. Looks like we've tilted, Harriet. Didn't see that one coming. How about a replay, how would that be? I'll stake you to a few credits. How about we just pull back the old plunger and give it another go, let her fly, and see where we end up? Yeah, let's do that. Ding-dong- ding, 1973. Nudge nudge, no thanks. Ring-a-ding-ding, 2012? Nudge nudge, forget about it. Click click, nudge nudge, dong-dong-dong, summer of 1965—now that's more like it.

Who's that smiling mom with the short, sassy hair, the relatively slim one in the pink one-piece and the fake Armani sunglasses, soaking up the rays, while her freckle-faced son with the peeling forehead frolics nearby in the sand? Why, of course, it's you, Harriet Chance, with adorable little Skipper! And it's no small wonder that you're smiling: you have so much to be happy about. Never mind that things are heating up in Vietnam, never mind those fires still smoldering in Watts, the future looks bright, at least from where you're lying right now, on the shores of Lake Washington, the sun beating down on your attractive face.

In a couple of weeks, Skip starts kindergarten, and you, Harriet, can finally rejoin the workforce, at least part-time. Oh, you don't have the same expectations this time around, heavens no. You're not looking to make a name for yourself, you just want a life outside of the house and a small measure of independence from your family. You miss the sense of purpose and the vitality of downtown. You miss lunching at the Continental. Most of all, you miss having a career, some other yardstick besides household cleanliness by which to measure yourself.

In a month or so, you'll have all that. Look at you, controlling your own destiny! You've done your work: typed those letters fastidiously (eighty words per minute; you haven't lost a beat), licked those envelopes, delivered those résumés (in person, dressing the part perfectly). You're giddy with anticipation. Any day now, that phone will start ringing and your new adventure will begin. Yes, it's been a fine summer, Harriet, a mild, uneventful, leisurely summer, full of barbecues and bikinis, ambrosia salads and dry martinis. But be honest, fall can't come soon enough.

Let's talk about the cherry on top: the fact that Bernard is behind this move one hundred percent. He kisses you on the head, pats your fanny, and says he's proud of your initiative. Yes, you married a decent man, Harriet. A little bossy, perhaps, a little stubborn, a little awkward with his emotions. But he's got his strengths, too: Dependability. Integrity. Good hygiene. He has your best interest at heart, he really does. And even when he's at his worst, his most ragged and impatient, when he storms out of the house and doesn't come home, he's always good for that rose in the morning. When has your husband failed to support you? In what decision has he ever failed to back you up? Yes, you might have asked for more, Harriet. But c'mon, he's no mind reader. It's not like you've been lobbying for your needs these past six years. No, Harriet, Bernard is not big on charm, he's not Cary Grant, not even Russ Tamblyn. And God knows, you won't find him leading the charge for women's lib, but he's as good, if not better, than most husbands.

And that, Harriet, is just one more thing to be grateful for as you hurtle toward thirty.

This is your life, going in a welcome new direction.

September 6, 1989
(HARRIET AT FIFTY-TWO)

And while we're discussing new directions in life, let's say we zip ahead (ding-dong-ding, flip-flip-flip) to the fall of 1989, where you're just getting settled in the banana belt, and the change is a welcome one. You adore your new home. Living in that drafty old house on the north end, you never dreamed of such an abode. The views are spectacular. Already, you can name every peak and ridge of the North Olympics, visible from your patio: Deer Ridge, Hurricane Ridge. Blue Mountain. That little one there is Lost Mountain. You could spend the rest of your days sitting on that flagstone patio, admiring the views, or in your spacious kitchen, chopping vegetables by the window, or tending to your spectacular garden.

So it hurts you just a little bit that Mildred never comes over. She's never been past the driveway, never seen the open floor plan, or the views, or seen Bernard in his natural environment, puttering in the garage, drinking coffee from an ancient thermos, listening to baseball on his transistor radio. The fact is, Mildred has only met him a few times in church basement over crumb cake, and that was before she stopped going to St. Luke's.

It's true, Mildred's house is grander than your own. A sprawling Tudor with trained ivy and a three-car garage. But then, Clark is a wealthy man. The one thing he hasn't bought much of the past thirty years—to hear Mildred tell it—is time with his family. The views from the bluff are equally spectacular, if not more so, than those from the Carlsborg house. So, you really can't blame Mildred for wanting to meet at her house (again), where you customarily sit on Adirondack chairs at the very edge of the bluff, the very edge of the world, it seems, two hundred feet above the strait. From this perch, you watch the occasional cruise liner or container ship inch past. You listen to the chorus of ravenous seagulls and the distant percussion of waves pounding the shoreline.

And you share, though not always in equal measure.

Listen to you eagerly confide in your new friend, as though you've spent the past thirty years marooned on an island, which is what being married to Bernard sometimes feels like. Let's face it, he's not a conversationalist. His idea of repartee includes a lot of hmphs and hmms, yeses and nos, nodding, sighing, and the occasional guffaw. He's from Lutheran stock. Midwestern. Conversing with Bernard reminds you of talking to your golden retriever, all those years ago. A tilt of the head, a wag of a tail, a snarl—it's about all you can reasonably expect.

So it's no small wonder you open up to Mildred. The fact is, you're sharing things with Mildred that you've never before given voice. Such as the fact that you still frequently think about the law, still cast yourself as the brilliant trial attorney in daydreams, dressed smartly in flattering business attire. That you sometimes think of your lost life, that you're still tracking that alternate you, as though your paths diverged at some distant juncture and went their separate ways.

The you that you could have become is everything that you're not: frank, unsentimental, uncompromising, to the point. The you that you could have been is funny, tough, adaptable. A little more like Mildred.

You sometimes wish you could ask the other you for advice, or guidance, or clarity, or at the very least a little perspective on the life you've muddled so badly. If only that other you could take you by the hand and walk you back through the misbegotten paths of your life—the botched decisions; the cowardly retreats; the circumstances you might have controlled, avoided, or otherwise been spared—to the very beginning, where it all started going wrong. You sometimes wish the other you could tell your story.

Wouldn't that have been something.

But let's not be maudlin, Harriet. We've so much to celebrate, as it stands! Your beautiful new home, all cedar and
sunlight, your faithful new friend, kind and considerate, and
let us not forget your reliable husband, as steady and predict-
able as the tides.

August 19, 2015
(HARRIET AT SEVENTY-EIGHT)

When Harriet regains consciousness, she's flat on her back, lying on the bed, ears still ringing. Propping herself up against the headboard, she stretches her legs out and stares dully across the room, registering nothing. Her first thought—before how could she possibly have been so oblivious or how could her entire life have been a lie—is how could another woman have possibly loved Bernard for that long?

And who was this dashing Bernard in the letter? And why did Mildred get him while Harriet got the bruised ego and the short temper, the irritable Scrabble opponent, the endless lectures on rust prevention. Since when had Bernard ever been "quietly strong"? Loudly strong, maybe; stubborn and determined, without a doubt. But quiet? And "troubled by the ways of his own heart"? What did that even mean, exactly? Headaches, yes. Back pain, frequently. Constipation, always. These things troubled him, and he was by no means "quietly strong" in bearing them. In fact, he could be downright mean. Taciturn. Worst of all, critical. When troubled by anything, Bernard was likely to turn the crosshairs of his anxiety outward, usually aiming them directly at Harriet. Grumbling and snapping about her constant nagging, her irrationality, her cooking, her lack of in-touchness with reality.

How was it fair that Harriet had given everything she had to loving a man who poured Miracle Grow on her character defects and meanwhile Mildred got some swashbuckling poet, just for the asking. "Irresistible"? How was that possible? When was it ever "effortless" to love Bernard Chance? Perhaps, in 1970, when he was still hale and hearty. But what about 1993, after the second botched back surgery? Or 1999, after the heart attack? Or 2013, when the real downward slide began? And where was Mildred when Bernard could no longer care for himself, let alone drive himself to one of their clandestine "couplings"?

Where did they do it?

How could they pull it off for so long?

How could she miss all those signals?

Did the children know?

Though the questions are manifold, and seem to multiply exponentially, Harriet begins to arrive, through the throng of complexities, at certain logistical reckonings:

The long days at work.

The off-site lunches.

The trade shows.

Later, the veterans' retreats and the coffee klatches.

And alibis aside, there was the arduous nature of their own infrequent intimacies and the springiness in his step upon returning from his veterans' functions. There were bouts of inexplicable cheeriness, which Harriet had always viewed as Bernard's way of apologizing for being an insufferable brute much of the time. All of it began to add up to what should have been obvious all along.

Then it hits her like a donkey punch to the stomach. Alaska. Just like Dwight said: Mildred tried to get Clark to take her to Alaska for years. Harriet's stomach rolls. This blasted cruise, it was never intended for her and Bernard, it was intended for Mildred Honeycutt and Bernard!

Air. Harriet needs air. Cautiously, she swings her legs off the bed, takes hold of her water bottle, and lowers herself to the floor, inching her way toward the veranda. Leaning on the rail, Harriet sips her water as the dazed bumblebee of shock buzzes slow circles inside her skull. When she runs her hand over her head with a sigh, the band of her Bulova watch gets tangled in her hair. She finesses it for a moment, trying to liberate herself before yanking it free. Tearing the watch from her wrist, she wings it overboard into the harbor.

Yes, Harriet, your cruise is yet to begin.

May 18, 1980
(HARRIET AT FORTY-THREE)

For months, the slumbering giant has been venting steam, opening fissures, seething restlessly beneath the surface. A bulge has formed on the north face. Magma roils in the depths. Lately, the town is quaking like Jericho.

And when Mount St. Harriet blows, look out.

Recall, Harriet Chance, the evening you catch your daughter stealing from you for the first time. You lost it, for sure. But before we judge you too harshly, let us consider your defense: the Chances are experiencing a rough patch, of late. Work is monopolizing Bernard's time. His hours are all over the map, even weekends. When he's home at all, he's distant, tired, less than inquisitive. Communication is breaking down. You have no idea what his life looks like outside the walls of your home. All you know is that those walls feel like they're closing in on you and that you're a long way from your idealized self.

Caroline is walking all over you lately. You have no control over her. At thirteen, she comes and goes as she pleases, where, you do not know. What you do know is that she dresses in rags and is developing a foul mouth to go with her incorrigible attitude. She's recently pierced her nose. She wears headphones wherever she goes, tuning out the world around her. Her new best friend, Kat, is the stuff of legend, you've never laid eyes on her. Caroline comes home smelling of cigarettes, raids the refrigerator, and leaves a mess in her wake. Bernard is too busy to notice these changes, and that's giving him the benefit of the doubt.

Even with Skip out of the house (though he's home every weekend and most evenings to ravage the kitchen, leaving a mess of his own), your entire life, it seems, is spent in service. And yes, you're being cheap with yourself, Harriet. It's second nature, at this point. Thank God for boxed wine, or you'd never take the edge off. Lately, you've taken to stowing the box in the lower cupboard with the crab pot you never use. The minute they're empty, you cart them to the garbage, stashing them under trash bags. You tell yourself you're getting them out of the way. What you don't know is that Caroline has been nipping at your stores.

In your defense, it's hard to blame you for losing your cool, when you've had such little help in raising Caroline. Bernard offers practically nothing in the way of guidance or discipline. Summoning his name doesn't even make for a good threat. "When your father gets home . . ." What? He'll read the paper? Turn on the news?

Anyway, before the defense rests, let's talk about motives (yours, not Caroline's). Caroline stole cash from your purse; she filched your mother's pearls, your diamond earrings from San Francisco. You caught her red-handed rummaging through your vanity. And after all she's put you through. After all you've done for her. One good slap in the face deserves another, right, Harriet?

Okay, so maybe you overreacted. God knows, you didn't mean to, God knows the pressure had been building for months, years, really. But twenty-four megatons was a bit much, don't you think? Slapping her not once, but twice, pulling her hair, scratching her, pushing her against the wardrobe— that was a bit much.

The verdict is guilty, the sentence suspended indefinitely. Now, everybody, please, just get over it, and move on with your lives.

August 19, 2015
(HARRIET AT SEVENTY-EIGHT)

After an hour of stewing in her anger, pacing the length of her cabin, trampling the letter with each pass, and glowering at the yogurt container as she visualizes all the things she'd like to do and say to Bernard and Mildred, Harriet should be exhausted. Her spine should be aching, her feet should be throbbing. But instead her heart is beating a furious war cry. Desperate for occupation, she looks about the cabin for something to clean or organize. Alas, the cabin is spotless.

Maybe food is the answer, maybe she ought to feed this ravenous temper. But she can't possibly go out in public, not in this state. Or can she? Yes, that's exactly what she'll do. Bernard and Mildred be damned. The Lord would see faithfully to their recompense. Whatever Bernard's intentions, this cruise belongs to Harriet now.

Without delay, she retires to the light of the tiny bathroom, where she rinses her face, her spirits inexplicably high, as she begins reapplying her mascara. There are crab legs to be eaten, wine to be drunk. This is an opportunity to rejoice in her suffering, to let the good Lord confirm and restore her spirit. But it's no use. Midway through her mascara, Harriet breaks down and begins to weep bitterly. Shunning her reflection, she lowers herself to the toilet and cries until her grief is exhausted, swallowing her agony in one hot lump, along with half a Vicodin.

Gathering her resolve, she continues her preparations for the launch party: fixing her makeup, sculpting her hair, donning her modest blue China dress, and applying a spritz of Tea Rose.

In the elevator, still slightly dazed, she's joined by two middle-aged couples.

"Apparently, they're mostly Filipinos," one of the men says. "They all speak wonderful English."

"That's refreshing," says the other man's wife. "So many of the Mexicans don't seem to speak the language."

The elevator empties onto the Lower Promenade, where Harriet hobbles across the atrium to the Pinnacle Bar as cruisers file into the party two by two. Though bold in its decor, the Pinnacle Bar is equally confused. While the bar itself is firmly committed to an art deco theme—the rich colors, the lavish ornamentation, the geometric patterns—the surrounding seating area looks like the lobby of a Red Lion, bland colors, faux wood, and outsized, shapeless furniture. Perhaps forty cruisers are in attendance, the bulk of them split between the bar and the buffet line, almost exclusively middle-aged couples in formal attire, cumberbunds and dress fronts stretched tight across their bellies. Suddenly Harriet feels frumpish in her shapeless China dress, with its high neck. Her pearl earrings, her floral perfume, her sculpted hair—all of it feels dowdy. Removing her compact, she inspects her lipstick. The sight of her wrinkled personage does little to improve her outlook. Maybe crab legs will do the trick.

And a half glass of wine.

Heading straight for the buffet, Harriet loads up and retires to a table near the piano. As if on cue, a wispy fellow in a powder blue suit begins to tinkle the ivories softly beneath the chatter of the party. Within eight or ten bars, Harriet recognizes the melody, though she can't put a title to it. A ballad, slow and sentimental, from her childhood, something from Mercer or Van Heusen, a melodic strain that conjures polka dots and moonbeams, summons held breaths and clasped hands and the streaming lights of a carousel. Innocence, that's what it invokes, a world uncluttered by complications, unsullied by irony, untouched by despair.

Harriet takes a tentative sip of her wine and sinks deeper into her club chair as the distant refrains wash over her. Nobody seems to notice when the number winds down to its conclusion, and the piano man slips seamlessly into the next, "My Funny Valentine." The wine proves to be a heady delight, coursing through Harriet's limbs and numbing her temples. Spreading her cloth napkin across her lap, she turns her attention to the crab legs. Gracious, but they are unwieldy things! Plying her cracker, she goes to work on a giant pincerless leg, clutching it fiercely every which way, spotting her dress with each futile attempt to penetrate the shell. It doesn't help that her hands are trembling, and the cracker won't grip, and the light in the Pinnacle Bar is murky at best. Before she manages to exhume so much as a shred of meat, she abandons the enterprise altogether.

Frustrated by the ordeal, she pushes her plate aside without sampling the minted peas. Instead, she empties her wineglass in a single toss. She's not at all certain she can get out of her chair without assistance, nor is she feeling in the least bit sociable, but the spell is broken. The longer she sits there with that heap of uneaten crab legs before her, hectored by thoughts of Bernard and Mildred, the more another glass of wine sounds like a good idea.

Powder Blue is tinkling his way toward the coda of "Moonlight in Vermont" when Harriet manages—just barely—to push herself out of the chair and set a wide base beneath her. Lightheaded from exertion, she leans momentarily on the table for support before casting off. Her legs are leaden for the first few steps, the world wobbling slightly on its axis. But once she begins wending her way through the crowded bar, reality begins losing its sharp edges, and the party assumes a slow-moving fluidity. Harriet feels surprisingly buoyant and, yes, pleasantly intoxicated amid the hive of surrounding activity. The air hums with snatches of disembodied conversation:

Keith and I prefer Panama, actually . . .

What a coincidence! I was an actuary . . .

That's what we used to think, but it's not . . .

No kidding?

Our youngest is only thirty miles from Sarasota . . .

Exactly. That's what I told him . . .

You should have seen the size of the mosquitoes. Like hummingbirds . . .

Yes, I'm sure, I looked in the black bag—twice. Did you look in your purse?

With the closeness of the room, and the bottleneck at the bar, it's difficult to discern who is standing in line and who is simply standing in place. Easing herself into the scrum, Harriet somehow finds herself at the front of the line in what seems like no time at all. Indeed, time itself seems compressed. Space seems endlessly navigable, if a tad blurry. Nearly everything is easier to endure under the glorious influence of white wine.

"Something white," says Harriet, surprised—though not discouraged—by the heaviness of her tongue.

"Chardonnay? Riesling? Pinot Gris?" says the young man behind the bar.

"I'm afraid I really don't know the difference anymore, dear."

"Do you like sweet? Dry? Fruity?"

"Sweet sounds nice," says Harriet, taking note of the boy's name tag: Rey.

"Here," he says, pouring out at small portion. "Try the Zin."

Harriet takes the smallest of sips and, finding it to her liking, empties the glass.

"Oh yes," she says. "That's nice."

Indeed, it's better than nice, it's a revelation! So crisp and sweet on the tongue! It's nothing short of delicious, the way the vapors rise up through her nostrils and tickle her brain. Oh yes, Harriet could get used to this all over again. Obligingly, the young fellow pours her a generous glass. "Enjoy!" he says with a smile.

"Thank you, Rey," she says, lazily. "I believe I will, dear."

The last bit sounds a little wobbly, even to Harriet's confused ear, though surely nothing to be concerned about. Sipping her wine as she turns, she splashes a little on the front of her dress.

"Oh dear," she says aloud to herself, then laughs without meaning to.

To her further delight, cruisers are proving themselves a considerate breed, allowing her a wide berth (some of them clutching their sleeves and lapels) as Harriet floats past.

Indeed, that's what it feels like, floating. Free at last from the aching, collapsing, structural demolition of her body, swept along in the current of cruisedom. Free from any reservations or inhibitions regarding the present or the future and, mercifully, free of the past. Oh yes, wine is a much better salve than anything the medical profession has ever prescribed. Even the Bible condones it!

Straight ahead, Harriet spots Sinta, the young woman from the terminal. What wonderful fortune!

"Sinta!" she cries, splashing a little wine on the woman's wrist.

"I beg your pardon?"

"It's me, Harriet Chance. From the terminal the other afternoon. I wanted to thank you once more for your help, dear."

"Have we met?"

"Oh, good heavens," says Harriet, waving it off and splashing a dab more wine. "My mistake, dear," she says with a listless tongue.

Harriet is slow to comprehend that the woman is bristling or that her bearded companion is aghast. By the time she stops slurring long enough to notice them, they're both staring holes in her. Suddenly the heat of embarrassment suffuses Harriet's face.

"Dear, have I offended you?"

In lieu of a response, the young woman simply turns her back on Harriet, her companion quickly following suit. At a stupefying loss, Harriet stands there, listing ever so slightly from side to side. Steadying herself, she raises her chin and her wineglass and decides to let the matter rest rather than risk exacerbating the misunderstanding. Like everything else, gauzed in a glass of sweet white wine, the situation is easily resolvable. Harriet simply moves on, sloshing her way back in the direction of the music, through the blur of voices.

Down to three and a half bucks in central Oregon . . .
Tatum says the reason the department won't let it go is . . .
Really? Limes, too? . . .
I heard it on NPR . . .

The crowd is threatening to overwhelm Harriet's senses. All the activity is distracting. The Pinnacle Bar is suddenly losing its fluidity. The thing to do is to get back to the cozy confines of her chair, back to the subtle refrains and welcome familiarity of Powder Blue and the songs of her youth. Perhaps she can conquer those crab legs after all. The exchange with the Asian woman has soured her to the prospect of mixing. Better to enjoy the food and entertainment.

Just as she'd hoped, the music has an immediate and soothing effect upon Harriet. The piano seems to give off warmth. Nested deeply in her oversized chair, wine refreshed, Harriet takes up the cracker once more, spreads her napkin in her lap, and proceeds to conquer the crab legs, at times abandoning the device in favor of a more aggressive and timeworn tactic—namely, that of twisting and coaxing the appendages with her bare hands, while alternately clenching them in the vicelike grip of her determined teeth, only dimly aware that she might be making a spectacle of herself.

Meanwhile, Powder Blue plays an up-tempo number Harriet

doesn't recognize before rendering a positively jaunty version of "Puttin' on the Ritz." Harriet will remember "Puttin' on the Ritz" as the final highpoint of the evening, the last glorious bit of grinning stupidity before Powder Blue begins playing the likes of "It's Always You" and "Night and Day," songs about the relentless singularity of a lover's affection. Always you—ha! Only you 'neath the moon—phooey! All those years "roaming through roses," all those "early twilights" and "caressing breezes," the whole time Bernard had Mildred Honeycutt on his mind, and heaven only knew what else. All along there were *three* 'neath the moon, not two.

Though emptier by the sip, her wineglass only grows heavier at each turn, and her blood seems to thicken as she sinks deeper into her club chair, where a darker inclination again takes hold.

Why Mildred? Her exotic cheeses? Her relentless soapboxing? Her hairy legs?

Certainly Mildred was no beauty, and goodness knows she could test Harriet's patience with her willful, irrepressible ways. Maybe that was her charm. Maybe it was because Mildred insisted on getting what she wanted. Even if it meant taking it from someone else. She insisted on satisfying her appetites, insisted on having her needs fulfilled. Maybe Harriet should have wanted more all along, maybe she should have demanded more of Bernard—more time, more consideration, more affection, more respect and freedom and dignity.

Harriet will not remember spilling the last of her wine on

the carpet, or cracking the stem of the glass on the edge of the table, or losing her pearl earring among the mess of crab shells. Not even dimly will she remember assaulting the ship's steward with a crab leg when he tries to assist her out of her chair, nor will she recall pitching sideways when, of her own volition, she attempts to extricate herself. No, Harriet will not remember being assisted out of the Pinnacle Bar by two somber crew members, nor being examined in the atrium by the ship's doctor, nor refusing to cooperate with said doctor. She will have no clue how she arrived back in her cabin.

October 1, 2013
(HARRIET AT SEVENTY-SIX)

You're still calling Deer Park the new cinemas, though they've been there for years. Look at that adorable old couple down front, the ones who brought their own popcorn: the little hunchback with the crooked lipstick and the scarecrow in the yellow pants and the marine cap. Look at them, arm in arm, gimping down the aisle, quibbling over where to sit. Why, it's Mr. and Mrs. Bernard Chance, looking to all the world like a perfectly matched pair. Yes, fifty-four years of cohabitation has the two of you behaving like bookends, perfectly matched opposing supports forced by proximity into cooperation. Really, that's no small accomplishment, Harriet, so go easy on yourself the rest of the way. The rest could have happened to anybody.

The movie is forgettable. As in, you couldn't remember it if you had to. Something Irish, or about Ireland, with a guy and a girl. But that's not the point. The point is, it's movie night, and the Chances are still making an effort late in life, though neither one of you likes to drive after dark, and my God, it's nearly ten dollars a ticket, even for seniors. Not to mention, you haven't seen a good film in two years (not that you can remember that one, either).

You can't remember getting old. You can't remember when exactly you started carrying umbrellas just in case, when you started scheduling your weekly hair washings, oversalting your food, or reusing zipper-lock bags. It happened gradually. The years just wore you away, dulled your edges, leached the color from your face, and flattened you out like river rocks. Again, not the point. The point—not to belabor it—is: you're old, sapless and enfeebled, especially Bernard, and yet, you're still trying, both of you. Still able. The world shakes its fists and rolls its eyes at you as you gum up traffic and slow down lines, and pay for every blasted thing in exact change, but by God, the Chances are not about to cloister themselves at home with their creamed corn and network television, no, they're still out there wrestling with the world at large, still going toe-to-toe with progress, still absorbing change, slowly.

But when you turn to Bernard in the glow of the credits, expecting to share his vague disenchantment with the evening's lukewarm cinematic fare, he looks dazed and frightened and something else: unreachable.

Dear, you say, are you okay?

Yes, yes, fine.

But his tongue is heavy, and he sounds a million miles away. And he's slow to rise from his seat, and it's not a cautious slow. You reason that he must have nodded off during the film (heaven knows, you almost did), and that the sleep state has left him disoriented.

On the trip home, in spite of timeworn custom, you do the driving, and he doesn't make a fuss over the fact. In the passenger's seat, he slumps in silence, and by no means a thoughtful silence. Something smells like urine.

At some point during that forgettable movie, your husband has forgotten a great deal more.

This is your life, Harriet Chance, falling off a cliff.

Only later will you discover that Bernard has had "an event"—let's call it a stroke—and that it's likely not the first. Only later will you learn about the plaque on his brain. But let's face it, Harriet. You hardly have time to take it all in, it happens so fast. In three months' time, the police will find him wandering Cline Spit in his pajamas. In six months, he will not remember your name. In a year, he won't remember his own.

August 20, 2015
(HARRIET AT SEVENTY-EIGHT)

Harriet is awakened rudely at 9:40 a.m. by the shrill crackle of the public address speaker heralding the *Zuiderdam*'s imminent arrival in the port of Juneau. Mired in a state of throbbing paralysis, Harriet is surprised to find herself sprawled atop the covers, still wearing her blue China dress, her lips chapped, her hair a mess, and one of her earrings missing. She remembers quite clearly everything up to the pleasant young bartender—the headiness of the wine, the hum of the party, the warmth of Powder Blue's piano. Beyond that, her recollections are so spotty, so scattered and diffuse, as to possess a dreamlike obscurity. Systematically, Harriet begins collecting these fragments of memory like shards of glass, trying to piece the previous night back together. There was some awkwardness with a young Asian woman, some trouble with crab legs. Broken glass. Some shouting. Dear God, was she rolling on the carpet at some point? There was some sort of scene, with onlookers. Crew members were involved.

The only thing standing between Harriet and a state of pure panic is her sorry physical state: her swollen brain beating in her head like a second heart, her stomach hardened to a fist, her shallow breath rising like ether fumes from her throat. She closes her eyes and stares at the back of her eyelids, desperately summoning sleep. But it's no use. The beating in her skull is too loud to ignore, almost loud enough to drown out the public address system still rattling on about docking procedure in Juneau. Slowly, she rolls off the bed and onto her feet, her stomach rising fast as she reaches for her water bottle. Dizzily, she stands at the bedside, squinting against the daylight until the room stops spinning and the PA ceases its squawking.

Shuffling to the bathroom, she washes down half a Vicodin, avoiding her reflection in the mirror. Clutching the grab bar, she lowers herself onto the toilet, where remorse settles in around her like a thick fog. Though her instinct is to crawl under a rock, she must flee this ship at the first possible opportunity. But for the next twenty-five minutes, the best she can do is sit on the toilet, clutch her face in her hands, warding off nausea and waiting for the Vicodin to take hold.

It's 11:00 a.m. before she feels human again, just in time to hear the rapping on her cabin door. Harriet sits perfectly still on the edge of the bed, holding her breath until, to her relief, the knocking ceases. But no sooner has it stopped than her door swings open and her cabin steward, Rudy, walks in carrying a stack of fresh towels.

"Oh, Ms. Chance. I thought you'd be ashore with the others."

"I was just freshening up, dear."

"Ah," he says. "How are you feeling this morning? You are well?"

"Fine, thank you."

"That's good," he says, averting his eyes. "We were concerned."

Harriet's ears burn.

"We weren't sure who you were yelling at," he explains. "And you wouldn't let us help you off the ground. We tried to get the crab leg out of your hand, but you wouldn't let go. The doctor kept asking you if were taking any—"

"Thank you for your concern, Rudy," Harriet interjects. "Actually, I've got a bit of a headache."

"Would you like me to come back later?" he says.

"Yes, dear. Would you mind?"

The minute Rudy leaves without replenishing the towels, Harriet finishes packing her handbag and doesn't bother with makeup. When the coast is clear, she steals down the corridor toward the elevators, where she promptly runs into another one of the young stewards, Wayan.

"Ah, good afternoon, Ms. Chance."

"Hello."

Is it Harriet's imagination, or is the young man hiding a smirk? Was he there? Is the whole crew talking about her?

"Going ashore?" he asks.

"Yes, dear."

"This fog is supposed to lift. You should take the Mount Roberts Tram."

This friendly exchange eases Harriet's mind immediately.

"Thank you for the tip, dear."

"Certainly," he says. "And if you get hungry, might I recommend Tracy's King Crab Shack on Franklin Street?"

"Oh?" says Harriet.

"The bisque and the rolls are superb." Wayan pursues. "That is, I mean, if you're not in the mood for crab legs."

He *is* smirking, the little hyena—she's sure of it!

A RUGGED LITTLE HAMLET of chipping paint, weather-beaten wood, and yellow brick, Juneau hunkers at the base of two gigantic mountains, half shrouded in fog. So sudden and precipitous is the terrain that the town has nowhere to sprawl. Even the hulking cruise ships ringing the harbor stem to stern—each one a city in its own right—appear tiny in the shadow of such grandeur. The little harbor buzzes with tourism. Everywhere Harriet looks she sees a guide in a wind-breaker handing out brochures, a sandwich board promising discounts, a taxi crawling past. Everywhere, cruisers gawk and gander and graze, clutching digital cameras and street maps, their sweatshirts emblazoned with moose and grizzly bears.

Though the fresh air enlivens Harriet somewhat, her head still throbs, and she suffers from an unquenchable thirst, which seems to rise up from the pit of her stomach. She doesn't dare eat, for fear she won't keep down the food. She doesn't dare wander too far, for fear she'll collapse. Still, her condition has improved markedly and, with it, the day's prospects. Indeed, the fog is just beginning to break, and the great craggy peaks are beginning to show themselves.

On a different day, under different circumstances, Harriet might be delighted. Here she is in Alaska. Think of the gift shops. The gem shops. The native art galleries. But if ever she's felt like she was going through the motions, it's now.

Maybe that had been her problem all along, going through the motions. Maybe that's why she failed to hold Bernard's attention all those years, or inspire his muse. Maybe her quiet steadiness and her stoic bearing had been dull. Maybe next to Mildred—spritelike, impulsive Mildred—Harriet had looked like a toadstool. And maybe Bernard, under Mildred's provocative influence, really had been a different man. Surely Harriet had failed to tap Bernard's potential. She hadn't pushed him hard enough, hadn't made him accountable for his flaws. Where Mildred had probably coaxed and challenged and dared Bernard, Harriet had accepted him, warts and all.

Though not a lover of heights, Harriet could use a little perspective. She stands in line for the Mount Roberts Tram.

Maybe from the top, her difficulties will look like trifles. The close quarters of the gondola do little to improve Harriet's discomfort. Nor does the vertiginous drop on all sides as the mountainside falls away. Halfway up, she's sweating. Her stomach is rising when it should be falling. Pressing her face closer to the window, she forces herself to focus on the little outpost of Juneau below, growing tinier by the minute through the parting fog. Hugging the shoreline along the narrow channel, a flotilla of cruise ships encircles the harbor.

Bernard would have liked this. She can't help but think it. Such thoughts are second nature. Even the most bitter of grudges cannot deter or distort their appearance. He would've liked the cables, the pulleys, the whole of the great gravity-defying apparatus that held them aloft and pulled them forward. He probably wouldn't have even looked down, but up at the seamless workings of the thing. That she can't stop seeing the world through Bernard's eyes, that she can't stop loving him in the face of his terrible deception, is at once maddening and heartbreaking.

Shuffling off the tram, she's glad for the air and proceeds not to the gift shop but the viewing area, where she stands off to the side by herself, leaning on the rail for support, gazing down at the scenery through tatters of fog as the line of red gondolas ascend and descend, disappearing beyond the first bluff, then reappearing near the base of the mountain. How is it possible that she can still love him?

The fist in her stomach redoubles. My God, what is she

even doing up here? With this hangover, under these circumstances. But even in her weakened condition, she cannot resist the pull of the gift shop.

She walks out forty minutes later, $186 lighter, with no less than four miniature totems, key chains for Caroline and Skip, and a lovely hand-carved Tlingit mask for herself. How refreshing to spend money heedlessly! Caroline is absolutely right: Harriet's cheap with herself. Starting now, she's going to spend money where she can. What's she saving it for? Posterity? How many years has she been wearing this blue overcoat? How many times has she wanted to replace that dingy patio furniture? It's time to spend money while she can.

On the tram down the mountain, Harriet stands with her back to the window, clutching the handrail with her free hand. She closes her eyes briefly as the car begins its descent.

"That mask was a little pricey, don't you think?"

She opens her eyes to find Bernard, at forty, standing directly across from her, cheeks sunburned to a crisp, forehead peeling, his nose a triangular blotch of calamine lotion.

"You!" she says.

"I know I've got some explaining to do. I tried to warn you."

"Don't bother. Really, Bernard. What on earth could there possibly be to say?"

"Maybe you're right."

"Go haunt Mildred, why don't you?"

Bernard winces.

"It serves you right, you know, that sunburn."

"I know it does. Look, I'm not here to make excuses. It wasn't you, it was me."

"Well, that's a big relief. Here I've been beating myself up for pushing you into the arms of my best friend."

"That's not what I mean. I mean, some part of me was, well, conflicted. I knew what I was doing was wrong, but somehow—"

"Oh, is this about your 'troubled heart'? Because I'd be really interested in hearing about this troubled-heart business. Since the Bernard I lived with didn't have a heart—more of a command center. And what about all this passion Mildred alluded to? The man I lived with was an automaton."

"She expanded me."

"While I washed your socks and ironed your slacks. Oh, this is outrageous, Bernard, really."

"I'm just trying to explain."

"What's to explain? It all seem pretty obvious."

"There were deficits to consider. Needs not being met. And I'm not blaming you, Harriet."

"I should say there were needs not being met! All those years, I never even had time to think of my own needs, and yet somehow you had time to go fulfill yours with somebody else."

"I was incredibly selfish."

"Just tell me, what was so bad about me, Bernard? Was I a bad lover? Was I too boring? Not impulsive enough? Because if that's the case, you might have said something before you went and had an affair for nearly four decades. You might have at least given me a chance to punch up my personality—dye my hair, read the Kama Sutra, something. Since when were you impulsive, anyway? You spent half your life with your face buried in a crossword."

"I hate crosswords. That's the thing of it. I just can't stop doing them."

"So you were hiding, is that it?"

"I suppose that's one way of looking at it."

"You took me for granted, Bernard, that's another."

"I got my punishment, though, in the end. In a way, you sort of exacted your revenge without ever knowing it, if you really start thinking about it."

Ashamed, Harriet turns partway toward the window as the tram clears the bluff and the ground falls away abruptly.

"I see," she says. "You're trying to strike some kind of bargain, is that what's happening?"

"I take full responsibility—for Mildred, too."

"Oh, is that so?"

"She tried to stop it, Harriet. Continually, she tried to stop it."

"Don't you dare defend her."

"She always thought the world of you," said Bernard. "And don't think for a minute that she didn't feel terrible about it, every step of the way. She hated herself and I hated my-self. But damnit, Harriet, she loved you, she really did. She understood you so much better than I did. She gave me more practical advice about how to—"

"Stop right there, Bernard. You're not helping your case."

"I haven't got one. Hell, if I were you, I wouldn't forgive me, either."

"Then what are you doing here?"

"I'm not sure what I'm trying to accomplish. And that's the truth. At first, I just wanted to be near you. The Continental was nice, wasn't it? That's all I wanted. The familiarity, the companionship, some chicken à la king."

"Stop," she says, turning her back on him completely. "Just stop talking."

Quietly, Harriet simmers as Juneau, its narrow harbor, its dirty little side streets, inches nearer. He's actually defending her! Unbelievable. Harriet can hardly control her rage. When the tram eases into the station, she turns back toward Bernard, ready to lay into him. But standing in his place is a family of five, eyes painstakingly averted, except for the youngest child, a boy of three or four, who stares unabashedly at Harriet as he empties his juice box with a slurp.

CTO Charmichael looks exhausted slumped behind his sturdy desk, his forgettable shirt rumpled, his thinning hair a little unkempt. The stack of files on his desk is perilously close to toppling.

"It appears, Candidate Chance—and again, I'm giving you the benefit of the doubt here—that you've been laboring under a slight misapprehension recently regarding Section One."

"Sir?"

"Specifically, with regard to the consequences of noncompliance, as clearly—dare I say, eloquently—outlined in Clause 1.4."

"Yessir. After our last conversation, I checked on that, sir."

"And?"

"You were right. Nothing will happen."

"Precisely, Candidate Chance. *Nothing* will happen. As in, nothing."

"With all due respect, that's not much of a consequence, sir."

"Oh no? Well, I beg to differ, Candidate Chance. Let us consider. Having been granted nearly a century to design and fulfill yourself, to have children, a wife, a lover, several careers, to have served your country, your community, your family, to have eaten and loved and slept and worried, *ahem*, in short, to have bumbled and mucked about 'down there,' as you refer to it, for nine decades, have you any idea of what nothing looks like? What it sounds like? What it feels like?"

"Uh, like nothing, sir?"

"That's it precisely. Of course, 'look' and 'feel' are misnomers, technically speaking. It's actually quite difficult to put into context. A few Greeks tried. But that was a while back, and they didn't get much beyond shadows and caves. I think we can agree that's not very far. Allow me to enlighten you: to experience nothing is to not exist, Candidate Chance. To never have existed. To never exist again. Period. To experience nothing is to be stripped of your every sense but one."

"Which one?"

"The sense of nothingness."

"So that's the punishment?"

"We prefer not to frame it punitively. We look at nothing as a choice. Just as we look at everlasting life as a choice."

"But sir, I can make a difference. I can be a comfort to her. At the very least, I can keep apologizing. Maybe she'll give in eventually."

"That may be the case. But it hardly matters in the big picture. And consider the risk, Candidate Chance. You're not just risking everything here—you are risking anything at all. Do you understand that?"

"Yessir, I understand."

"I hope you do, Chance. I'm rooting for you, I really am. We all are. I hope you won't do anything rash. Go with the program, son. Reap the benefits. You've been given an excellent opportunity for transition here. Don't squander this one by getting mired in the past."

"Yessir, I'll try not to."

"You'd best not, Candidate. Or you'll have nothing to pay."

February 14, 2014
(HARRIET AT SEVENTY-SEVEN)

Here you are at seventy-seven, Harriet, still kicking, still marking your days with Bernard, though you haven't had movie night in four months. Indeed, overnight, your life has once again become what you've been fearing: cloistered. You're desperate for diversion, restless to leave the house, but that means taking Bernard, the 140-pound infant, along. And if you thought baby Caroline was a terror, think again.

Probably not a good time to remind you that it's Valentine's Day as you spoon-feed Bernard Cream of Wheat. No big surprise that Bernard has forgotten the feast of St. Valentine, seeing as how he's forgotten his address, his middle name, and apparently how to swallow, as evidenced by the dollop of gruel oozing its way down his stubbled chin. A few things he hasn't forgotten, a few useful platitudes upon which he leans all too heavily in his new version of conversation: "Speed will kill a bearing faster than an increased load." "You wanna prevent rust? Vinegar." And of course: "They used to call Okinawa the gray pork chop."

It's enough to drive you crazy, Harriet, literally.

You understand that caring for someone can be a thankless job. You were a parent, after all. You don't expect gratitude. But the least he could do is cooperate. The least he could do is not rap you on the side of the head when you attempt to wrestle his pants on, or bite you when you're trying to feed him.

Let's talk about the ugly truth, Harriet: There are mornings, and this is one of them, when you want to smother Bernard with a pillow, mornings when you're sure you're capable. There are moments when your hatred for him is a blind red impulse you can neither control or contain. You scold him viciously when he fouls his pants, throws food, rails against your every kindness. Times like these, you can no more sympathize with Bernard than you could sympathize with an egg salad sandwich. He's a thing. You have no earthly idea what, if anything, you are to him.

It doesn't matter that his condition isn't his fault. It doesn't matter that the hellish degeneration worming its way through his brain is in itself punishment enough for a dozen men. It doesn't matter what water has passed beneath your bridges the past half century. Living with him, caring for him, sleeping with one eye open, is a torture worse than physical abuse.

Half the time he doesn't recognize you. The other half he's erratic, often hateful, sometimes violent.

And it's not just pillows. Oh no, Harriet. You fantasize about clubbing Bernard senseless like a harp seal. Pushing him down stairs, in front of UPS trucks, off of cliffs. Only halfheartedly do you fantasize, of course. It doesn't matter that you'll never act on these impulses, it doesn't matter that they're just aberrant manifestations of extreme frustration and grief, the sort of thing that any caregiving manual would caution you against, they are sick and unforgivable, and you hate yourself for these thoughts.

Face it, you're out of patience, Harriet, out of pity, out of will, out of gas. Totally without the desire to go on living like this. And yet you keep going. Is it your unflagging sense of duty? Your unwavering commitment to service? Or is it just instinct? Surely, it's not your love of Bernard, because this is not Bernard we're talking about here. Bernard, as you once and always knew him, has been replaced by a human Brussels sprout.

What you ought to do, Harriet Chance, is strap Bernard into bed by the armpits, as your father once strapped you, then retire to the bathroom and soak your feet. What you ought to do is ask for help. Self-care, Harriet—they talk about it at the Partners of Alzheimer's support group in the basement of the Calvary Chapel. The one you don't go to.

March 17, 2014
(HARRIET AT SEVENTY-SEVEN)

All of which, in retrospect, Harriet, begs the question (and apologies for bringing up a sore subject), but where the hell is Mildred Honeycutt now that her lover of forty years is sitting before the television in a loaded diaper, with tapioca running down his chin, convinced that weatherman Steve Pool is hatching a plot to kill him?

As it turns out, Bernard would also like to know the whereabouts of Mildred. "Darling, you're confused," you say. "It's me, Harriet, your wife."

"You're not Mildred."

"No, I'm Harriet."

"Where the hell's Mildred?"

"I have no idea. Probably at home."

"Who are you?"

"I'm your wife. I'm Harriet."

And using one of the few tools in your belt (not that it ever works), you reach for the wedding picture (must be the twentieth time in two days) and hold it out to him, pointing out Bernard in his two-button tuxedo and you in your mother's wedding dress.

"Who the hell is this?"

"That's us, on our wedding day."

"Whose wedding?"

"Ours—yours and mine. See."

He blinks at the picture, uncomprehendingly. Blinks again, still nothing.

"Where the hell's Mildred?"

April 14, 1973
(HARRIET AT THIRTY-SIX)

And speaking of Mildred, now that we're starting to put it all together, do you happen to remember where your husband was on April 14, 1973? I'll give you a hint: he'll still be there in two days, when you celebrate your fourteenth anniversary alone.

Yup, Bernard is in Philadelphia instead of at home for the occasion of his daughter's birthday.

No, you didn't have any help with the arrangements, it's true. But c'mon, Harriet, it was a kid's birthday party, not the inaugural ball. Since we're being honest with ourselves, just admit it, you practically phoned in your daughter's birthday party. Not to say, you weren't harried throughout the debacle.

Half drunk on white wine, you burned the cake, then frosted the damn thing with your hands as though you were slathering grease on a ball joint. You forgot to invite half the class. You even forgot to tell Skip, who was at a baseball game. The paper napkins didn't suit the occasion. You accidentally bought diet soda.

And that's before the party even started.

Look at you, Harriet: your tank is two-thirds full by the time guests start arriving, and that's when you begin calling them all by the wrong names.

You forgot to put out the snacks.

The living room is a mess.

There are no beanbags for the Toss-Across, no pins for the donkey.

And your replacement donkey tail is—*ahem*—rather obscene-looking.

Not your best work, Harriet.

But it gets worse. After the cake has been eaten, at least those portions that are edible, after the oversized, distinctly elliptical tail with its bell-like tip has been pinned on the donkey (thankfully, not between its hind legs), you come up three candles short in the end.

You knew you forgot something at Food Giant!

Epic fail, Harriet. But before you go too hard on yourself again, just remember who Bernard was with that moment when Caroline finally blew out those three candles. That's right, he was with your future best friend, Mildred

Honeycutt, eating pie, and for all you knew, stroking her hairy leg under the table.

Now that we're starting to put it all together, now that we're really starting to see things as they were, how about a big "Fuck you, Mildred Honeycutt"?

November 4, 1942
(HARRIET AT SIX)

And since we're on the subject of sixth birthday parties, let's talk about your own, Harriet, what the heck? Not to compare, but your mother doesn't drop any balls in making the arrangements, oh no. This party actually looks like an inaugural ball. Tropical fruit punch in the crystal bowl (and no, that's *not* canned pineapple), a two-tiered German chocolate cake from Borracchini's, gift bags with tin whistles, rubber elephants, and homemade brittle wrapped in cellophane, and nothing that looks even remotely like a donkey dick.

Twenty-one children and forty adults attend, including your best friend, Miriam Addleman. Unlike Bernard, your father is not in Philadelphia. He's right there, lighting the candles, snapping the pictures, smiling at his pride and joy, if not checking his watch occasionally.

But for all the pomp and circumstance, for all the little frilly details upon which your father spared no expense, your sixth birthday party, for lack of a better word, sucks, Harriet.

Though you've come out of your shell considerably and are developing something resembling a confident voice, you are not a social animal. If given the choice, you still lean toward invisibility.

Not gonna happen, not today. After the games and the gifts and the singing, after you've blown out exactly six candles, and your father has cut the cake, and you hunch greedily over your towering wedge of layered chocolate and coconut, your mother renders you all too visible.

"For heaven's sake, Harriet, don't take such big bites," she says in front of practically everyone. "You think you might've learned your lesson by now, Little Piggy." Then, turning to Miriam's mother, she explains: "The child has a weakness for food. She nearly choked to death when she was a toddler, you know."

You still feel the familiar heat of shame coloring your cheeks as you swallow your last big bite of birthday cake, which tastes less like German chocolate and more like an act of defiance.

A little later in the party, as the kids are ramping up for

sugar-induced chaos, and the parents, just beginning to show their liquor, stop caring, the whiz kid, Charlie Fitzsimmons, takes you aside.

"That wasn't very nice of your mom," he observes.

"Daddy calls you the whiz kid," you say.

He smiles. Twirls a few locks of your hair between his fingers. "That's right," he says. "The whiz kid. He's always got your back."

And then he tells you the story about how he was big and awkward as a kid, in someplace called Quincy, and his friends called him Charlie Fatzsimmons, and his father called him Fatz, and the lady from the Chinese grocery called him *Ju,* which meant "pig" in Chinese.

"You know Chinese?"

"Only a little."

"Could you teach me?"

"What I know, I suppose."

After talking to Charlie, you feel better—a lot better, actually. He even smuggles you an extra piece of German chocolate cake and sits with you while you eat it by the water heater.

August 20, 2015
(HARRIET AT SEVENTY-EIGHT)

By the time Harriet is shipboard again in Juneau, the worst of her hangover has passed. She's exhausted, but pleasantly so, as she surrenders her boarding card at the checkpoint without a hitch.

"Welcome back, Ms. Chance. Did you enjoy Juneau?"

"I did, dear."

"Excellent. Watch your step."

Such is her state of fatigue that even the thought of Mildred cannot arouse Harriet's ire as she progresses turtlelike down the carpeted corridor, clutching her Tlingit mask and her tiny totems. She can't wait to get to her cabin. That footbath never sounded better. A cup of herbal tea from room service. Maybe the other half of that Vicodin. For the first time, this cruise is beginning to sound restful.

In spite of a shaky hand, Harriet wields her card key with aplomb and pushes through the door. She nearly jumps out of her orthopedics when she sees who's waiting there. Perched on the love seat, hunched over Mildred's letter, Caroline looks up, flush with excitement.

"Jesus, Mom," she says, setting aside the letter. "This is seriously fucked up in like a really big way."

"Put that down. And please don't talk like that."

"I mean, I knew Dad was a creep, but this takes the cake."

Harriet snatches the letter off the coffee table. "You might have warned me you were coming. Why are you here?"

"I never left Vancouver. You just seemed, I dunno, just . . . the whole thing made me nervous. I was worried. So was Dwight."

"Dwight? What does Dwight have to do with anything?"

"So I got a flight."

"How did you manage that?"

"My phone."

"Dear, I appreciate your concern, but you can't afford that, can you?"

She averts her eyes toward the yogurt container on the dresser. "Skip had miles."

"And how did you get aboard? How did you get into my cabin?"

"I made some calls."

Harriet looks at her doubtfully.

"Skip made some calls."

"To whom?"

"The cruise line, I guess. And Dr. Ritchie. He faxed a note."

"What could Dr. Ritchie possibly have to do with any of this?"

"Never mind that. Mom, this is nuts. Dad was fucking Mildred for like half his life. Jesus, no wonder he was never home."

"Stop talking like that, please."

"Well, shit, Mom. This is seriously screwed up."

"Do you think I need you to tell me that? I know screwed up when I see it, Caroline. My goodness, I'm looking right at it." Harriet regrets the statement, immediately.

Caroline stands, turns toward the veranda. "I see. Fine."

"I'm sorry," says Harriet, setting her bag down. "I didn't mean that. Sit down, sweetheart. It's been a shock, that's all."

"Fuck, I guess so," she says, resuming her seat. "You're telling me you had no clue?"

"Caroline, *please,* stop using that language."

"Oh get over it, Mom. You're not that old-fashioned. You really had no idea? All those years?"

"I didn't. My God, Caroline. Don't you think if I . . . of course I didn't."

"How is that even possible?"

"Do you think I don't feel like an idiot? Just imagine."

"Well, I'm not a bit surprised, actually."

"Good for you. As it happens, I was, Caroline. And quit being so hard on him. We're all 'fucked up,' as you like to put it."

"Why are you defending him?"

"I'm not."

"Unbelievable. After all you did for him."

"He did his share for me, you know. And for you, too."

"See, you're doing it again. It's like a habit with you, Mom."

"You're right, it is. And a tough one to break. Oh, but please darling, I'm so tired. I apologize, it was a terrible thing to say. You're not screwed up. I'm the screwed-up one."

Harriet takes her coat off and throws it on the bed. "So, I take it you're coming along?"

"Yeah. That's okay, right?"

Harriet looks at Caroline's measly purse. "What will you wear?"

Once again, Caroline averts her eyes. "I'll figure it out in Skagamalack or wherever. I'll buy a sweatshirt with a moose on it. And a bathing suit. This will be fun, Mom, you watch."

"Do you have money?"

"Skip's wiring some."

"You could always ask me, you know."

"No, thanks."

"Caroline, things are different now. You're in a different place. If you need money, I can always—"

"Mom, I appreciate it. But you've done enough. Really, I don't want your money."

"Why won't you ever let me help you, dear?"

"Won't I?" Caroline stands and walks to the sliding door. She's about to step out onto the veranda when she turns back to Harriet.

"Honestly, I don't get it, Mom. You find out your husband was cheating on you for like . . . fuck, half your life, and you don't seem that upset about it. Christ, not only do you forgive him, you defend him. You never went that easy on me, that's for sure."

"I know, I know. I made you go to summer camp. We've been over that. I apologize, Caroline. My God, if I could have possibly known that I'd be hearing about it forty years later, I would never have made you go."

"Oh, please. Like this has anything to do with summer camp."

Suddenly the room is beginning to sway, and it's not the *Zuiderdam*. Harriet tries to ease herself backward onto the bed, and misjudges the distance, just enough that she nearly loses her balance.

"Jesus, Mom, are you okay?"

"Yes, I'm fine. Just worn out. Dear, could you hand me the water bottle on the coffee table, please."

Caroline uncaps the water and hands it to her, looking genuinely concerned. "Are you sure you're okay? How's your back?"

"Fine," says Harriet.

"You look pale. Should I call someone?"

"Heavens, no. Thank you," says Harriet, kicking off her shoes. "I think I'll just rest my eyes. Make yourself at home, dear."

And no sooner has Harriet swung her legs onto the bed,

rolled over onto her side, and closed her eyes than sleep begins to seep heavily into her bones.

"Just holler if you need me," she hears Caroline say.

"Yes, dear." She can barely get the words out.

She hears Caroline walk to the bathroom, shut the door, and turn on the shower. Within seconds, Harriet is sleeping like iron.

May 7, 1955
(HARRIET AT EIGHTEEN)

Look at you, Harriet, the week before senior prom, all decked out in champagne taffeta for your dress fitting. Look at you, chin up, back straight, as your mother sits nearby impatiently, offering unsentimental commentary.

Terrence Osier is to be your date, he of the debate club, captain of the basketball team, and your parents roundly approve. He comes from a good family, father's a circuit court judge, mother's a Nordstrom. They're members at both the University Club and the Tennis Club. The truth is, in spite of his pedigree, Terrence Osier doesn't do much for you, with his dirty blond cowlicks and his smug self-assuredness, but then, most boys don't do much for you.

Your father is sparing no expense on the dress. He's treating this prom like some kind of debut. You've been starving yourself for three weeks (with more than a little coaching from your mother), and it's working. You feel good about yourself, even though you sense something vaguely wrong with this state of affairs. The truth is, the pressure you feel to be thin is mostly external. Who are you starving yourself for, Harriet? Not Terrence Osier.

The A-line design is supposed to be slimming. But it's all wrong, your mother says. The hem is too high. Your kneecaps look like frozen game hens. Your ankles look fat. When the woman tailor, who does not disagree, brings the hem down, you look squat. It's enough to exasperate your mother.

You've been absorbing it your whole life, Harriet. Every time you pick up a fork or form an opinion. You're sick of it, sick of wondering what is wrong with you that you can't please your mother. Like a wicked den mother, she nits and picks and criticizes you constantly, so much that you're convinced she doesn't even mean to, that it's a compulsion. Why does she seek always to improve you, as though it's her life's work? And why do you take it to heart? Is it because you already know that you'll never be all that you could have been? Because you'll never be able to tell your own story the way you want to tell it? Because you haven't got the courage? Isn't it enough that your father believes in you, Harriet? Your father, who, according to your mother, is naive, in spite of all appearances, and doesn't understand the ways of the world. Your father who's been blinded by his rose-colored glasses. Your father who wants to see a princess in every warthog. Your father who has no idea what it is to be a woman. You may be his princess, he may think the world of you, he may pull some strings for you, honey, but you'll always be a woman in a man's world, mark my words.

And nobody wants a girl with fat ankles.

Okay, so not the first time your mother's been wrong, oh no, not by a long shot. Turns out, Terrence Osier doesn't give a whit about fat ankles, Terrence Osier is primarily interested in breasts. He spends forty minutes after the dance, all chin and elbows, groping to get at your ample pair in the backseat of the green-and-yellow Chevy Bel Air his parents bought him. But not before Terrence wins a debate on the subject, which is—let's be honest—brief, not that you have any interest in being fondled, rather because you always aim to please. The fact is, any sort of petting makes you vastly uncomfortable.

Alas, the tiny expensive zipper on that dress only buys you five minutes. But lucky for you, Terrence is far from adept at the art of unclasping brassieres (not as fast as some—*ahem*—with a little more experience), or you might not have escaped with what was left of your dignity.

The takeaway here, Harriet, is that there's nothing wrong with you. You've got big ankles and an unhappy mother. You're versatile and absorbent. You can do a lot with that, as a woman, or a paper towel. So, what are you waiting for, child?

This is your life, Harriet, go out and get it!

September 17, 1965
(HARRIET AT TWENTY-EIGHT)

Whose dexterous fingers are those, shuffling sprightly through legal files, gliding over writs and motions, line-dancing across that IBM Selectric like they were born to it? Why, they're yours, Harriet Chance—that is, *Ms.* Harriet Chance, as you like to be called around the office. Yes, not yet thirty, you're finally downtown again. Generating income (not that Bernard's salary is in any way insufficient), exercising your independence, using your powers of critical thinking toward some end beyond laundering, cooking, and cleaning.

You're catching up with the other you. Telling your own story, or getting closer, anyway.

It's your second week back at work, and you've hardly

skipped a beat. Despite your six-year absence, a new office, and a whole new set of protocols, you're proving yourself nothing if not adaptable, and it feels good.

It feels great, in fact.

No sooner have you left your domestic station than the world is suddenly a bigger place, full of sights and sounds and actions you cannot predict. No matter that your duties are purely administrative. No matter that your function is invariably to serve. Your refreshing enthusiasm, confidence, and efficiency are a boon to the whole firm.

Charlie Fitzsimmons says so himself.

Okay, asking Charlie for a job wasn't the plan. Not even plan B or C. The other you would never have done that. But let's face it, they're not just handing out jobs to twenty-eight-year-old homemakers, six years removed from the workforce. In fact, not one of those meticulously prepared résumés got you so much as a callback. I guess the interesting thing here, the question we may want to be asking is, why didn't you call upon your father's network? God knows, he could've scared something up for you. He's Harriman Nathan. He's got his own table at the University Club. There's a YMCA gymnasium named after the man. At sixty-nine, his name is still the first one on the marble slab. So, why not go to him for a job instead of Charlie Fitzsimmons?

Admit it, pride is only part of it. There's something else, Harriet, something way down deep. Something you've struggled for twenty years to understand, a cruel and inexplicable magnetism that almost feels like duty. You could probably take this thing apart piece by piece and understand it, but that is something you're not ready for or are unwilling to do.

Ahem. Moving on.

To Uncle Charlie's credit, he's honored that promise he made you in your parents' hallway half a lifetime ago. And what's more, age has apparently mellowed him. There are no strings attached to this favor. The strings, mercifully, appear to have been cut. While he shares with you the same old confidence and familiarity, he's been a perfect gentleman, so far. Not so much as a slap on the fanny. Hard to believe, really. Sick as it sounds, you can't help but worry that you're no longer attractive.

Six months, a year from now, everything will look a lot different, Harriet. But let's not get ahead of ourselves again. Let's just linger here for a moment. Let's not talk about the ways in which your job spreads you thin on the home front or how your domestic responsibilities are not diminished, only compressed into fewer hours. And let's definitely stop talking about fathers and uncles and husbands, and the power they hold over you.

No, let's just enjoy the moment, breathe deeply of this last, albeit brief, reprieve from your domestic bell jar.

August 20, 2015
(HARRIET AT SEVENTY-EIGHT)

Across the aisle from the window, on the starboard side of the Lido buffet, Harriet picks around a shrimp cocktail, gazing distractedly to the east, where the verdant coastal range runs like a spine. They're still hundreds of miles from the glaciers, yet Harriet can see the evidence of their patient, grinding retreat in the canyons left yawning in their wake.

"The food isn't bad," says Caroline, inhaling her fettuccine.

"You look as though you haven't eaten in weeks."

"Pardon me for enjoying my meal."

"That's not what I meant."

Caroline spools some fettuccine. "Mom, sometimes it's best not to comment. Didn't you learn anything from all those lawyers?"

"Touché," Harriet says.

Things are going pretty smoothly between them, all things considered. Beyond a bit of the usual touchiness, Caroline seems resolved to making the best of their time together in captivity. The truth is, Harriet's glad for the company, happy to have an ally. Yes, she's had a rough go with her daughter, but it hasn't all been bad.

"Let's do something fun," she says.

"Like what?"

Harriet fishes out her reading glasses, unfolds her daily planner, and begins scanning the checklist. "Well, it looks like there's a comedian in the Vista Lounge. Clayton Somebody-or-other."

"Ugh."

"I'm with you," says Harriet. "Most of them aren't very funny. Last week, I saw a young man on *The Late Show* who had a parakeet for a partner. Every time the comedian would say something, the parakeet would chime in with 'Squawk.' That's what she said. 'Squawk.'"

Caroline guffawed.

"Oh, c'mon, Caroline."

"Well, it's kind of funny, Mom. At least when you do the parakeet."

"Look here," says Harriet. "We can still catch the tail end of the digital-photo-sharing workshop if we hurry."

"No, thanks. And I'm not sure I'd classify that as fun."

Undaunted, Harriet goes back to the list. "At six, there's a signature cocktail tasting in the atrium."

Caroline frowns. "Yeah, great plan, Mom."

"I'm sorry, dear, I don't know what I was thinking."

The mere suggestion of a cocktail has Caroline palming the tasseled monkey's fist at the end of her key chain. Harriet doesn't know how many years of sobriety the knotted little rope represents, but she knows that every day has been hard won for Caroline.

Watching her, Harriet's heart sinks a little. Something about that little knot always makes her sad, maybe the way it's burnished from all of Caroline's nervous handling.

"I'm proud of you, Caroline. You know that."

"It is what it is, Mom, that's all."

"I know it must get hard."

"Squawk. That's what she said."

"I'm being serious here, Caroline."

"Fine, Mom. Thank you. You're right, it's hard. And most days I don't even see the point. But I mark them off, one at a time. What am I preserving?"

"I know the feeling," says Harriet.

"Do you?"

"Let me ask you this, Caroline: how much time did you spend with your father near the end?"

"Fair enough," she says. "Maybe you do know. Anyway, it's not anything I want to talk about." Even as she says it, the hand with the monkey's fist retreats under the table.

"I'm sorry, dear. I mean for ever turning my back on you."

"Mom, really, I don't want to talk about it."

A third voice breaks in, as Kurt Pickens, the giant from

Kentucky, appears at the end of the table, clad in another sleeveless T-shirt, clutching a plate of buffet fixings—from prime rib to sushi.

"Y'all mind if I join you?"

"Why, of course not, sit down," says Harriet. "This is my daughter, Caroline. Kurt was kind enough to help me locate my cabin and carry my luggage," she explains.

"The pleasure was all mine, Ms. Chance. Kurt Pickens, Owingsville, Kentucky," he says, extending a hand. "Pleasure to meet you, Caroline."

Kurt squeezes into place at the table, picks up his fork, and promptly devotes himself to the task of eating with a steady, businesslike comportment (the prime rib being his first order of business).

"Are you enjoying the cruise?" Harriet inquires.

"Mmph," says Kurt with his mouth full. "Little bit, I guess."

"Juneau was pretty wasn't it?"

"Not bad. Lot of mountains. Don't reckon I could live there," he says, stabbing a potato. "Too foggy."

Throughout the meal, Harriet continues to solicit conversation from Kurt while Caroline shoots her looks intended to let her know that she's being rude. Finally, Caroline can't hold her tongue.

"Jesus, Mom, let the poor guy eat."

"Dear, I'm just being friendly, I . . . Kurt, I hope I . . ."

"No, no," insists Kurt, forking a California roll. "Hell, I don't care. I'm from Bath County, where a buffet likes company. 'Course Donna Mae could never abide a buffet. Donna Mae liked the finer things."

"Caroline," says Harriet, piloting the conversation swiftly away from Donna Mae. "Mr. Pickens says there are some Chances in Kentucky."

"Trash, mostly," he says, glancing over his fork at Caroline. "No relation of yours."

"Nice of you to say so," says Harriet.

Kurt is beginning to warm up a little. And while Harriet would not characterize him as cheery, he is disarming. Where he might lack a little polish, and a couple of sleeves, he's thoughtful. And much to his credit, he makes no further references to Donna Mae. Throughout dessert, he illuminates the cultural benefits of something called the "Ole' Cornfield," and something else called the "I-64 Motorplex."

In the elevator, Harriet tests the water.

"What did you think of Kurt?"

"What do you mean? He's fine. How should I know?"

"I'll admit, he's a little rough around the edges. But he has a native politeness, don't you think? And he's actually quite attractive for a larger man. A bit like Zero Mostel."

"Wait a minute," says Caroline. "You can't be serious. Mom, whoa. Are you trying to hook me up, here? He weighs like four hundred pounds. You don't even know the guy."

"He could lose it. You changed your habits, didn't you? Get him on a diet. Clean him up. Put some sleeves on him. He's really quite nice when you get beyond superficiality."

"Is that really as good as you think I can do, Mom? Seriously? You must think I'm a real loser."

"I don't think you're giving him enough credit."

"He drinks, Mom. What else do I need to know? And anyway, Jesus Christ, who says I'm looking to meet anybody?"

"I didn't see him drinking anything."

"Why do you think his cheeks are so red? That's a drinker's tan."

"I thought he was embarrassed about belching."

"Not to mention he's probably diabetic and about fifteen minutes away from a heart attack. Thanks for looking out, Mom, really. But if I ever start dating again, I'll let eHarmony take care of the profiling."

Back in the cabin, Harriet sheds her clothing in favor of a nightgown and climbs into bed without removing her makeup. Snapping on the lamp, she dons her glasses and begins flipping through one of her complimentary glossy magazines. Caroline kicks her shoes off and lays down on the love seat, where she picks up the TV remote and flips through the channels for ten or fifteen minutes. Unable to find a sufficient distraction, she snaps off the television with a sigh.

"I think I'll go up to the observation deck or something. You wanna come?"

"I'll stay here, dear. Don't forget your key."

Caroline slips back into her shoes and fetches her purse off the dresser. "And Mom, do we have to look at the ashes? Can you move them or something? And please, do yourself a favor, throw away that damn letter."

The minute Caroline shuts the door behind her, Harriet regrets staying. Caroline is right, it's suffocating. There's simply no escaping Bernard and Mildred.

Though Mildred was a comfort to Harriet after Bernard's passing, always on hand with a casserole, it now occurs once again to Harriet that Mildred might have been a lot more helpful during the precipitous decline of Bernard's mental health, considering she'd spent decades loving the man. Surely, Mildred might have picked a less convenient time to abandon him.

"He deserved a better ending," Mildred had said at the wake as Harriet scattered ashes beneath the lilac.

At the time, the statement had sounded almost like an accusation, one Harriet felt she'd earned. She'd set them both up for failure. Now Mildred's words strike a discordant note. Just where the hell was Mildred to help improve Bernard's ending? Where was Mildred fifteen times a day when Bernard observed, as though for the first time, that "while a tactical victory for the Japs, the Coral Sea was a strategic victory for the Allies"? Worse than the diapers or the vacant expressions or the spoon feeding of apple sauce had been the tedious repetition of "We used to call Okinawa the gray pork chop," "Speed will kill a bearing faster than an increased load," and "You wanna prevent rust?—Vinegar."

"What can I say? She didn't have your patience."

Harriet turns to find Bernard beside her in bed, his hair thinner and whiter on this occasion. His lips, receding slightly, are dry; his chest, pale and sunken. Little tufts of white hair have taken root in his ears.

"She had a mustache, too," says Harriet. "In case you hadn't noticed. And she was downright fickle. Not to mention downright pushy with her opinions. And pretty unreliable when you get right down to it."

"We've all got warts, Harriet. Hell, I was made of warts, you know that. I didn't deserve either of you."

"Is that supposed to make me feel better?"

"The point is, I was a terrible husband, a terrible person. I see that now, clearer than ever. I was thoughtless and inconsiderate, and I made bad decisions, big ones. And what's worse, I stuck to them like General Custer. I was an absentee father, a tight ass, an unreasonable judge, a liar, a cheater, a—"

"You weren't that bad."

"But I was."

"Just let it go, Bernard. Don't make me defend you again."

"Aw, but Harriet, c'mon. You're too damn forgiving of me. You always were. Give me what I deserve for once."

"You got what you deserved, remember?"

On that note, they retreat into a dense silence. Harriet stares up at the ceiling and listens to the sound of her own shallow breathing. He's right, she thinks, she's too easy on him.

"Are you real?" she says at last.

"You're talking to me, aren't you?"

"Why didn't you come sooner?"

"It's hard to explain, honey, trust me. It wouldn't help you to understand, anyway."

"How long do you plan on hanging around?"

"Probably not long."

Again, they fall silent. Shifting slightly on her back, she feels the graze of his arm hairs. She turns to him and looks him right in the eye.

"Am I going to die?"

Bernard doesn't answer.

"Well, am I?"

"Of course you're going to die, Harriet."

"Soon?"

He rolls over on his side so that his back is facing her.

"Tell me," she says.

He reaches over and turns off the lamp. "It's getting late."

"What do you mean? For heaven's sake, it's only seven ten."

Just then, the door opens as Caroline returns from the observation deck. Cheeks red, hair windblown, she looks around the cabin.

"Who were you talking to?"

"Just the television, dear."

"Seriously, Mom, are you sure you're okay?"

"Just sleepy, dear."

November 4, 1966
(HARRIET AT THIRTY)

Ring-a-ding-ding, it's your thirtieth birthday, Harriet Chance, let the party begin! Bernard has risen to the occasion, once again proving that he's a thoughtful husband, in addition to being a good provider, an excellent mechanic, and a prolific shoe shiner. He's arranged a sitter for Skip. Dinner reservations with the Blums at Canlis! A table by the window, overlooking Lake Union. Filet mignon and Chianti by the bottle. Why, just seeing Bernard in a suit and tie ought to be worth the price of admission.

So, why so glum, beneath that courteous smile, birthday girl?

Is it because you couldn't find a thing to wear, not a stitch of clothing that would fit over your blasted stomach, swollen as it is to the size of a bowling ball? Because your ankle straps are cutting off your circulation? Because after barely a year back on the workforce, another unplanned pregnancy has sunk your prospects for a career?

That's part of it.

But there's more, isn't there? Something darker troubles you, Harriet, as you and Margaret retire to the ladies' room for a powder. Something you could never confide in Margaret. Or Bernard. Something you'll never tell Mildred. Something you'll have to confront by your lonesome. As a matter of fact, it will be forty-eight years before you will confide the information to anyone.

But let's put things in perspective here. It's not the end of the world. That's still coming, Harriet. No, in the big picture, what troubles you probably won't matter.

Unless you make it.

So c'mon, birthday girl, turn that frown upside down, and start counting your blessings! Things won't turn out so bad. It's just a little setback. So you're gonna lose your administrative job, so what? Really, you should be thrilled. It's not like you're barefoot. Go on, take a nip of that flask Margaret carries around in her purse. That ought to help. Hey, it's 1966, smoke a cigarette in the bathroom while you're at it. Hell, you can smoke it at the table.

The thing to remember, the thing not to lose sight of, the thing your mother has been trying to tell you forever is this: Quit being so selfish, Harriet. You're not worth it. Quit being ambitious, quit wanting so much, you don't deserve it. Once and for all, quit casting yourself as the victim. Just be a good woman, and bear the load life hands you. Put on some lipstick and live a little. And order another martini while you're at it.

This is your life, Harriet, the first day of the rest of it.

August 21, 2015
(HARRIET AT SEVENTY-EIGHT)

By the time Harriet and Caroline stake out a window seat and unfold their napkins, the public address has sounded its call for Skagway and the Lido deck is beginning to empty. The mighty *Zuiderdam* slows to a crawl as the tiny borough of Skagway appears off the port side, a little slab of a town wedged deep in the gullet of a steep valley. Above and beyond, loom the great snowcapped domes of the Yukon.

"You're sure you won't join me for the train excursion?" says Harriet. "I've got two seats."

"I've gotta pick up Skip's wire and buy some clothes. Find some other stuff."

"Then why don't I just forgo the train and come along with you on your errands?"

"No."

"It'll be fun."

"No, Mom. Definitely not."

A little crestfallen, Harriet turns toward the window.

"Mom, don't be that way."

"Lord knows, you don't need me slowing you down."

"It's not that."

"What is it, then?"

"Look, I just won't have you missing that train trip. It sounds amazing. Much better than slogging around this frontier looking for a fax machine. I can meet you afterward. We'll go to some shops and grab a bite."

Within the hour, Harriet has taken her place alongside the railroad tracks next to cruise facilitator C.J. and fifty or sixty other cruisers. From this vantage she can see straight through the center of town, which could be a film set, with its lone, wide avenue dressed up in gold-rush glory, its wooden storefronts, facades painted cheerfully in reds, and pinks, and yellows, brimming with tourists.

The trip to White Pass Summit does not disappoint. By the midway point, Harriet has deemed the excursion well worth the $130 she paid in advance. The vintage railway coach is both comfortable and tasteful with its burnished wood and expansive windows. And the scenery is nothing less than breathtaking. A panorama of jaw-dropping grandeur: of gorges and glaciers and cliffhanging corners. Ice fields, thawing meadows, and alpine lakes splayed fingerlike between

the broad-shouldered mountains. Even the names are evoc-
ative: Bridal Veil Falls. Dead Horse Gulch. Inspiration Point.
And oh, how Bernard would have loved the tunnels and the
towering wooden trestles, the feats of engineering, of jobs
done right, how he would have adored the noisy workings of
the train itself, the thrum of the rails, and the clatter of the
coaches.

Harriet finds it virtually impossible to entertain anything
but reverence for the rugged splendor of the Klondike. She
can't remember the last time her imagination was so free
to wander. The vastness of the place is profound. Here at
last is the perspective she's been looking for these past few
days through the myopia of her emotional and psychological
distress.

Harriet's lone regret is the vacant seat beside her, its empti-
ness so dense that it seems to occupy space. Is she weak to forgive Bernard so readily, weak to let him off the hook so easily?
Is she pathetic—gazing out the window of that bygone train
as it carves its way through what was once the last frontier—
to wish that she could once again summon the ghost of her
husband?

Of course she is.

Like a prayer answered, Harriet turns to find Bernard
seated beside her, paunchier and slightly jowlier than his last
incarnation. His Brylcreemed hair is receding, his eyebrows
are nearly growing together in the middle.

"Don't get too cozy over there, Bernard. I finally enjoyed

myself today in spite of everything else, and I don't need you badgering me with apologies."

"What can I say, doll? I like our little talks. Hearing your voice, it's like old times."

"I guess it took death to make a conversationalist out of you. The Bernard I remember could go an entire evening with little more than a few grunts from behind his newspaper. Anyway, what makes you think you can waltz in here and act so familiar? You must think I'm pretty quick to forgive."

"Quick to forget, anyway. Besides, you're polite—it's your good breeding. How do I look, honestly? Do I look fat?"

"No."

"See? You didn't even hesitate."

"Well, you don't. You look healthy."

"Admit it, you miss me."

Harriet averts her eyes.

"You do," says Bernard. "The quiet little things that didn't add up to much: watching TV together, stringing Christmas lights, beating me at Scrabble."

"That's not fair, and you know it. Nothing is what it was. It's like my entire past has been rewritten. And for the record, you were a terrible Scrabble opponent. Always hurrying me. Grousing about your lack of vowels. Double-checking my math. Rolling your eyes every time I consulted the dictionary. You were incorrigible."

"Fair enough. How's Caroline?"

"Why don't you ask her yourself?"

"I've tried. She won't communicate with me. That's the thing. They gotta be willing."

"Well, she certainly doesn't have the highest opinion of you. She says you were a bully."

"Some people are not easily persuaded. Maybe my style was a little bullish, I see that now. But I got results."

"Don't take it personally," says Harriet. "She's says that I favored Skip."

"Did you?"

Forced to consider, Harriet is not pleased with the verdict. Hadn't she always been slower to comfort Caroline? Even as a baby, Harriet had let Caroline cry more than she'd ever let Skip. She'd weaned Caroline at barely six months, whereas Skip might have nursed until his freshman year of high school if he hadn't weaned himself at two. Of course she favored Skip.

"Yes," says Harriet. "I guess I did."

"So did I," says Bernard "Well, there you go. The rest is easy."

"Nothing is easy between Caroline and me, you know that."

"What could be easier than apologizing?"

"You don't seem to understand. She wants to remain at odds, I'm convinced."

"Stubborn," says Bernard. "Like her mother."

"I wouldn't be so sure. You're the one who refused to use the bypass for seven years. Winding around that damn marina, driving four miles out of our way to get to the grocery store."

"That damn bypass killed the town."

"We were the last house on the peninsula with a rotary phone."

"Perfectly good phone."

"If it were up to you, we would have used a telegraph."

"Now you're exaggerating."

"You wouldn't eat shrimp if I put a gun to your head."

"Not meant for consumption—"

"—unless," she chimes, in perfect unison with Bernard, "you happen to be a narwhal."

Harriet blushes at the familiarity. How can she still feel at home with a man she no longer knows? It vexes her that she takes comfort in his usualness.

"Why didn't you ever tell me, Harriet?"

"You're a fine one to ask that question."

With a great hiss, the train grinds to a halt in Skagway. There's Caroline, waiting by the tracks.

When Harriet turns back to Bernard, she finds only a vacant seat.

June 9, 2014
(HARRIET AT SEVENTY-SEVEN)

Look, Harriet, you've done an admirable job caring for your husband the past eight months. You've tried—really hard, you've tried. If you could ever manage to attend the support group, you'd know the task is nearly impossible. You'd know that you're not alone. You'd know that your futility and rage were perfectly normal. You'd know that caring for someone with Alzheimer's is one of the most difficult and demanding jobs in the world. Nobody's good at it.

If you could only see clear to read the stack of materials Dr. Ritchie provided, you'd know that you're only in the middle stages. Yes, Harriet, it gets worse! You'd know you have to take better care of yourself, even as your partner's disease swallows your every available resource. You'd know you have to step away from it all sometimes, ask for help. Call Mildred, call Skip, call the Department of Social and Health Services. The Department of Aging and Disabilities. There are outside resources, Harriet, plenty of them. Most of them have acronyms.

No, they can't help your husband remember your name, but they could give you some tools to work with. They could refer you to some home-care possibilities. They could probably send somebody out to walk you through your options, some kind of social worker. Gracious, Harriet, you live in the banana belt, the state capital for elder care. A mecca for the blue-haired set. Swing a cat, hit a medical specialist. Alzheimer's is as common in Sequim as athlete's foot.

Then, why oh why oh why won't you ask for help? Exactly what are you trying to prove?

Maybe it's time to say when, Harriet. Before Dr. Ritchie sees the bedsores on the backs of Bernard's legs, before he finds the string of bruises along Bernard's inner thigh. Funny, how they're shaped like the Aleutians in a crescent, each yellowing island the mark of an offending finger.

You lost it, Harriet. Just for a split second while you were bathing him, patiently trying to scrub the mess from between his legs, the one leftover from his recent accident in the post office, where he would not be ushered out of the lobby without making a scene. The clerk stared at you with pity and revulsion as you shepherded him out the door, cursing and swinging his arms. In the car, Bernard kicked the rear-view mirror clean off the windshield. Twice, he tried to grab the wheel on the drive home, and you had to fight him off. You kept your cool the whole time, Harriet. You dealt with the situation competently. You managed to settle him down, get him home, undress him with the usual difficulty, take off his diaper, and coax him into the bathtub.

Not bad.

But when he began to splash you and curse you all over again, that stifled rage came rushing up from the center of you in an instant, and Mount St. Harriet blew her top again. Maybe not twenty-four megatons but a pretty good blast.

It was an isolated event. It happens. Take your own advice, and let it go, Harriet. Quit remembering the confusion in his eyes, the helplessness in his prairie-blank face, as you dug your fingertips into his soft flesh.

Yes, it's time to say when, Florence Nightingale. Before Skip and Caroline and Dr. Ritchie intervene. Before they sit you down in your own living room and tell you how it's going to be.

You better hurry, though, because they're knocking on the door.

August 21, 2015
(HARRIET AT SEVENTY-EIGHT)

Caroline looks positively delighted standing there by the tracks, clutching two oversized shopping bags. She's wearing a lovely Cowichan sweater cinched at the waist, featuring twin orcas, one over each breast. The sweater couldn't have come cheap, especially not in a tourist trap like Skagway. Happy as she is to see her daughter in high spirits, Harriet can't quite overcome the suspicion that Caroline is somehow taking advantage of Skip's generosity.

"So, how was it?" Caroline asks, offering her an elbow.

"The views were stunning," she says. "Your shopping was a success, I see. The sweater is adorable on you."

Harriet suggests that they double back and drop Caroline's bags in the cabin, but Caroline insists she's famished.

Dining at the Harbor House, they both order the salmon, and Caroline displays her new clothes for Harriet while they wait for their entrees. A polar fleece pullover in a flattering blue. A stylish pair of bootleg jeans. A black one-piece bathing suit. The more genuine enthusiasm Caroline expresses over these purchases, the less Harriet worries about Skip. He can afford it. It's sweet that he's doing this for his sister. When was the last time Caroline went shopping anywhere but Ross or T.J. Maxx? When was the last time she even seemed to care what she was wearing? It occurs to Harriet that she's not the only one with a history of being cheap with herself.

The salmon is overcooked and Harriet doesn't even recognize the vegetable. There are spots on the water glasses. Everything is overpriced. But nothing can dampen the spirits of mother and daughter as their dinner conversation unfolds easily. No trampled toes or raised hackles along the way. Caroline's monkey's fist never leaves her purse.

Afterward, Harriet insists on picking up the tab, tipping a hair over twenty percent.

"Look at you," Caroline chides. "Big tipper."

"Oh, stop it," Harriet scolds. But the truth is, she's pleased by her daughter's approval.

Arms grazing, they stroll back down Skagway's main thoroughfare, as the sun dips below the mountains and the dusky air assumes an autumnal chill. The little shops begin to light up, and somehow the town seems less rugged and suddenly more quaint.

"I'm glad I came," says Caroline.

"Me, too," says Harriet, clutching her hand.

They continue their leisurely pace, past the Gold Digger Mine and Dine, and Prospector's Cafe, soaking up the manufactured charm. Passing the hokey mercantile, a half-dozen more gift shops, and the train museum, they arrive, pleasantly flushed, at the monstrous hull of the *Zuiderdam*.

Upon their return to the cabin, Caroline is still energetic.

"They've got karaoke in that lounge upstairs. What do you say, Mom?"

"Dear, I couldn't eat another bite."

"No, it's music. People sing along. It's fun."

Exhausting as the mere thought of venturing out is, Harriet can't disappoint Caroline.

"Just give me a few minutes to freshen up, dear."

Caroline changes into a fresh blouse and her new jeans. Side by side, in the tiny bathroom, they apply their makeup and finesse their hair. By the time they're finished, Caroline looks ten years younger and ten years happier. Harriet looks like a dried fig.

"You look nice," says Harriet.

"You, too, Mom."

But the long walk down the Rotterdam corridor to the elevator bank is beginning to take a toll on Harriet. Her neck is starting to throb. The balls of her feet ache. She can actually feel her mental focus softening.

The interior of Northern Lights certainly doesn't help. The

club is even more incoherent than the Vista Lounge, as though Dorothy Draper and a color-blind sultan have been set loose in the place. The host, DJ Raj, is a swarthy young man clad in pointy dress sandals and a fez, shiny pants of indeterminate material, and a billowy shirt with a leather drawstring.

"Next up, give it up for Cindy, yo. Cindy in the hoooouuusse!"

An inebriated bottled blonde of forty-five, with a suspicious tan, wobbles to the stand in an immodest blouse, seizes the microphone from Raj, and promptly announces, "People say I look like Stifler's mom," just as a chorus of synthesized strings takes flight beneath her.

No sooner do they find a table and start perusing the non-alcoholic beverage selections than Caroline stands up, as if to go to the bathroom.

"Dear, are you certain you don't have a bladder infection? You just went five minutes ago."

"I forgot, I've gotta e-mail Skip real quick, let him know everything is okay. I told him I would."

"Didn't you just phone him in Skagway?"

"What can I say, Mom? He's concerned."

Though the news ought to annoy her, it pleases Harriet to know that Skip is thinking about her. He may be his father's son, he may not visit enough, he may take Harriet for granted much of the time, and yes, her little Skipper underestimates her, always has, but she's never had reason to doubt his genuine concern, or question his motives. Not like Caroline has given her so many occasions to do.

"Please hurry back, dear," she says.

In Caroline's absence, Harriet is forced to give the music her attention, with nothing but a flat club soda to distract her. And frankly, it's giving her a headache. It's not that the singers themselves are terrible (though, make no mistake, most of them are completely tone deaf and can't keep time to save their lives), it's not even the canned elevator arrangements that aggravate her. It's the material itself that grates on Harriet. The compositions are inane. They just don't possess the same pluck and punch as her beloved standards. Often, the lyrics suffer from imprecise grammar. In some cases, they don't make sense at all. Mosquito, libido, anything for a rhyme.

No, it isn't Harriet's imagination, this new music cuts corners whenever possible, suffers from the yawning, butt-scratching torpor of the overfed teen, sprawling on unmade beds in the glow of television sets. Where timeworn sentiment, even pith, was once the objective of well-turned lyric, a simple "yeah yeah" would now suffice. A rhyme. An arbitrary allusion to insects.

Harriet sips her warm club soda and tries to tune the music out, though each performance commands her attention anew. Cindy's appetite for center stage cannot be sated. Her forehead glistens under the bandstand lights, the neckline of her blouse plunging farther, as she caws and screeches like a disgruntled raven. But worse still is the imprecise grammar of DJ Raj, yo. He may as well be speaking a foreign tongue with all his "shiznits" and so forth. With each song, Harriet's mood deteriorates further. And she can't even order a glass of wine to take the edge off.

By the time Caroline finally returns, twenty-five minutes later, Harriet can hardly contain her annoyance.

"Sorry, Mom. It's such a pain to log on. It takes literally forever."

"Which is how long I've been sitting here alone."

"I said I'm sorry, Mom."

And just like that, they're back to their old ways. All the goodwill they created throughout the past two days is beginning to erode.

"And just what did you tell Skip that was so important that you left me sitting here by myself all night?"

"I told him that we were fine, Mom. That we were having fun."

"Mmm," says Harriet, folding her arms.

"Well, aren't we?"

Something in Caroline's expression softens Harriet. She could say something else about the thoughtlessness of Caroline's actions, about the terrible music, about the warm club soda, about her aching neck and back and feet. She could say something about Caroline hijacking her cruise and taking advantage of Skip. But something has changed. For the first time in years, Harriet can see a glimmer of hope in her daughter's eyes.

"Yes, dear, of course we are."

December 25, 1972
(HARRIET AT THIRTY-SIX)

Look around you, Harriet, at the sights and sounds of a Chance family Christmas. See the handsome Norway spruce festooned with tinsel and lights. Hear old Bing belting it out on the hi-fi. Feel that crackling fire, smell that tangy ham. And look at those four felt stockings dangling above the hearth, the ones you yearned for so long ago. You've much to be grateful for, Harriet.

So why are you so disenchanted? Is it because you think you've wasted your life? Because you think the other you would be ashamed of you?

No offense, but why do you even bother sneaking to the kitchen to spike your eggnog, when everybody, even your five-year-old—especially your five-year-old, as it turns out—

knows what you're up to? For this is the only mother Caroline has ever known: at turns, gloomy and erratic, often heavy of tongue, frequently rheumy of eye.

Be honest, Harriet: you don't even know why you're crying in the kitchen. You have zero emotional clarity at this moment. Your emotional self has no borders, no shape, no horizons. You can't tell rage from sadness, anymore. You're lost at sea emotionally.

That's it, have another eggnog.

The fact is, Harriet, you're a certified drunk. Everybody sees it but you. Pretty soon, you'll catch on, and once you do, you'll do a serviceable job of hiding this fact, but mostly you will overcompensate for it.

Bernard, by degrees, has gone into hiding the past two years. Really, you can't blame him for withdrawing. You've made yourself opaque to him. In less than three months, he will have a chance encounter in Philadelphia that will change his life for the better. Yes, Harriet, had you been a little more proactive, and a little less in your cups, things might have turned out differently in Philadelphia: a certain hairy-legged two-timer might not have stolen your husband's heart. But then, maybe you wouldn't care about that, either. Maybe at this point, jealousy is outside your atrophied emotional range.

At what point did you lose control of your life, Harriet? When did you start hating yourself? When did you decide to start slowly killing yourself, and why? Maybe the answer is at the bottom of that highball glass.

Or not.

Oh, go ahead and make another, Harriet. But stick with me here. This part has a happy ending. Sort of.

As you're slumped at the kitchen table, trying to reconcile your anger with your despair, five-year-old Caroline comes to comfort you. Actually, she's just ferreting out another Christmas cookie when she walks in and finds you there, weeping inconsolably for no discernible reason.

"Come here, honey," you say.

Reluctantly, she inches toward you, expressionless. You reach out for her hand and pull her close to you. Warily, she submits. You clutch the child to your chest until she has no choice but to surrender to your embrace.

"Mommy's sorry," you say.

The girl says nothing.

For five minutes, you hold her captive.

"It's not your fault," you tell her.

Again, she says nothing.

You clutch her even tighter. You rock her like a baby, sobbing into her shoulder, as she stands there stiffly, silently, no doubt confused.

Ho ho ho! Merry Christmas, Harriet! All is calm, all is bright.

August 22, 2015
(HARRIET AT SEVENTY-EIGHT)

I n the Lido buffet at breakfast, Harriet wipes her mouth and pushes her Greek omelet aside as she scans her daily planner.

"What about aqua aerobics with lifestylist Rocco at ten?"

"Sorry, Mom. I've got stuff to take care of."

"You've got all afternoon. C'mon, let's get some exercise. We've done nothing but eat for two days."

"It's a cruise, Mom. That's what you do. You're supposed to gain five pounds. You go and enjoy your activities, I wanna get this stuff out of the way."

"Well, what is it? Maybe I can help."

"That's okay, relax. Enjoy your cruise."

"What if I don't feel like relaxing? Let me help."

"No, Mom, I've got it."

"What is it? Is it work?"

"Some of it, yeah. Look, Mom, it's just some stuff, we'll talk about it all later, okay?"

"Mm, I see," says Harriet. "I understand, of course, I get it. I'll give you your space, I'm sorry." She folds her planner and stuffs it in her purse. "You always needed your space. You and your father."

"Mom, it's not like that. We'll hang out later."

"I'm getting on your nerves."

"No, actually. You're not. I'm having a great time. A lot better than I expected. Really."

It's a left-handed compliment, but Harriet will take it.

"Well, so am I," she says. *"Actually."*

They exchange sly smiles.

"Good," says Caroline. "We'll do something fun later. And Mom, do me a favor: take it easy. I mean with the exercise stuff, be careful. Don't overdo it."

"You act like I'm going to fall and kill myself."

"Well, shit, Mom, can you blame me? Look, have fun. Just be careful, that's all I'm saying. Promise?"

"Promise."

After breakfast, they go their separate ways.

Arriving at the pool punctually, Harriet is unaware that she's been entertaining any expectations regarding lifestylist Rocco until she sees him standing poolside, clutching a yellow float noodle: four foot six, and Asian. Not that the young man is unattractive. Somehow she'd just expected someone brawnier: a blue-eyed Neapolitan, with thick, dark brows and chiseled biceps. But what he lacks in stature, Rocco compensates for with spunk. And it's contagious. Who knew water walking could be so much fun? They (eleven women and a Swedish fellow in what amounts to a thong) kick, and punch and make water waves, working their abs and hamstrings and buttocks, their quads and glutes and joints, while Rocco remains tirelessly upbeat all the while, despite the fact that the poor dear practically has to tread water in the shallow end.

When it's over, Harriet feels jelly-legged but energized. Easing her way out of the shallows, she's already famished again.

Scarcely has she seated herself in the buffet than the hulking figure of Kurt Pickens appears at the head of her table.

"Y'all mind if I join you?"

"There's just me, dear."

Though Harriet notes with satisfaction that today Kurt's T-shirt has sleeves, it poses a rather offensive question in bold print. Namely, WHAT THE HELL ARE YOU LOOKING AT?

"Just lost my nut up in the casino," he says. "Couldn't buy a hand."

Without further ceremony, he lowers himself into his seat and sets methodically to work on his mashed potatoes.

"I'm sorry to hear it, dear."

"Ah, well," he says. "Sun don't shine on the same dog's ass every day. This whole damn thing was Donna Mae's idea," he observes, stabbing a forkful of sausage. "Hell, I wanted a flat-screen TV. But Donna Mae, she was bent on seeing Alaska. I said, 'Well how about someplace decent, like the Caribbean?' You know, Hawaii or whatever? But that was Donna Mae. Willful as a damn bloodhound." He forks a meatball and pops it in his mouth. "Unfortunately, not as loyal."

"I'm so sorry, dear."

"Reckon she thought she deserved better," he says, chewing. "Somebody fitter, more adventurous. Somebody named Garth in a white convertible." He stabs another meatball.

"Oh, Kurt, that's awful."

"Yeah, well," he says, waving it off with his forkless hand. "Once she lost the weight, it was the only logical conclusion for us."

"I doubt that's the case."

"It's the case, believe me. She made the right move. This Garth in the white convertible has a lot on the ball. Some kind of investment banker in Lexington. Plays tennis. Drinks martinis."

"That's all superficial," says Harriet.

"Look at me," he says. "What do you see?"

"Honestly?"

"Yeah, why not?"

"I see a young man in a rather off-putting T-shirt who talks with his mouth full."

"What else?"

"A young man who could stand to lose a few pounds around the middle if he doesn't want to invite heart disease.

But a handsome one nonetheless. And quite knowledgeable—particularly in the arena of motor sports. Overall, I see a young man with a lot of potential, with his best years still in front of him."

"Well, that's not what Donna Mae saw."

"The hell with Donna Mae," says Harriet. "Become an advocate for yourself."

"Okay," says Kurt. "I'm a three-hundred-and-forty-pound recently divorced guy on a cruise by himself. I drink too much, I'm generally antisocial (though I'm afraid to be alone), I have a gambling problem, and it turns out I'm scared of mountains."

"Well, that's not so bad."

"Okay. I lost my house in the divorce, Donna Mae fought me for custody of my cats, then had them put to sleep, I hate my job in wholesale plumbing supply, I wanna kill my boss, and the truth is, I don't care if I wake up tomorrow morning, although the breakfast buffet is decent." He carves out a bite of mashed potatoes. "Oh, and I'm impotent. So where do I go from here?"

"Glacier Bay," says Harriet. "That's where you go from here. Then Ketchikan. But with a new attitude, a new way of looking at things."

Kurt spears half a sausage and pilots it to his mouth. "Go on," he says.

"Maybe you go to the gym instead of the casino next time. They've got wonderful facilities here on the boat. You'll feel better about yourself if you do something about your situation. You might start by putting that fork down."

Still chewing, Kurt lowers his fork slowly. There's nothing left on his plate but a smear of mashed potatoes and gravy.

"Oh, dear, I've offended you, haven't I?"

Picking up his empty plate, he stands. "I'm going back for some of that pork loin. You need anything?"

June 21, 2014
(HARRIET AT SEVENTY-SEVEN)

Well, Harriet, it's come to this. You've lost control of your life. Or Bernard's life, anyway. Probably a blessing, don't you think? Really, it ought to come as a relief, when you get right down to it. At least they're not trying to take your house. At least they're not coming for you.

Bernard sits stiffly on the sofa, fully clothed, awaiting the toast that is not forthcoming, while *Good Morning America* unfolds quietly on the television, though neither of you is watching it. You never do. You just like the company.

No matter how you entice Bernard to move from one activity to the next, one place to another, he's uncooperative. Like Bartleby, he'd prefer not to, though Bartleby was never this cantankerous. Still, you have no choice but to try to move him. On at least five occasions already this morning, you've informed Bernard that you're taking him to the Old Mill for breakfast. Your favorite, remember? A white lie he will never remember.

"Where's my toast?" he wants to know.

Yes, he loves toast, though he chokes on it frequently.

It's early morning and the fog off the strait has not yet lifted when Caroline and Skip arrive in Skip's SUV. Caroline opens the back door for you and Bernard.

"Who's she?" Bernard wants to know.

"That's Caroline."

"Caroline who?"

Here you are, Harriet, in the backseat, clasping Bernard's hand in yours, on the drive to Sherwood Arms. Three and a half miles, and it feels like you're driving to Spokane. You've dressed Bernard nicely, though dignity is lost on him. He'll foul the white dress shirt the minute anyone tries to feed him. He'll probably foul the diaper, too. But it's no longer on you, Harriet. Admit it, as terrible as it sounds, it's a relief.

God, but it happened so fast. How is it even possible?

"Where the hell are we going?" he wants to know.

Look at Caroline fondling her monkey's fist in the passenger's seat.

Look at Skip, fifty-five years old, gripping the wheel at ten and two, just like his father taught him.

At reception, you try to distract Bernard. But he doesn't give a damn about any goddamn aquarium, does he? He wants his toast. Where the hell are we? he wants to know.

You shepherd him past reception. The walk down the corridor is a long and toastless journey. Finally, you arrive at number five. There's a clipboard affixed to the door. A placard with two macramed carrots that says HOME SWEET HOME.

It's so nice, you all say. Look at the view. They've thought of everything, haven't they? And the staff is just lovely. Oh, look at the television, Bernard, just look at the size of it!

But you're really just talking to yourselves, aren't you? Because for all Bernard knows, he's in Donald Duck's living room with three complete strangers. All he knows is he wants toast. Bad enough to yell about it.

But you can see it, Harriet, a look in his eyes, an alertness, as if somewhere behind the disease, behind the scar tissue, behind the fog of disassociation, Bernard is all there, he's just lost his ability to communicate. Like somebody turned off his volume. You're certain he can see everything that is transpiring with crystal clarity, and he can't do a goddamn thing about it.

Somebody, please, get the man some toast.

August 22, 2015
(HARRIET AT SEVENTY-EIGHT)

When Harriet returns from the buffet, she finds the DO NOT DISTURB sign dangling from the door handle of her cabin. Inside, the shower is running, and steam seeps in from beneath the bathroom door, fogging the windows. The cabin is a disaster area. In less than forty-eight hours, Caroline has taken over the room. Not the organized type by nature, her parents' zealous attention to tidiness only seemed to encourage Caroline's slovenly ways, as though her messiness was an act of defiance—one of many—that would last a lifetime. Her possessions, though few, are scattered widely, from the heaping coffee table to the unmade bed, where her dirty underwear is on display.

Instinctively, Harriet begins straightening the cabin, determined not to begrudge her daughter. She gathers the new sweater and blouse, hanging them in the tiny closet. Fishing the underwear off the pillow, she drops them in Caroline's canvas bag. She smoothes the sheets and makes the bed before turning her attention to the chaotic coffee table, where from beneath Caroline's jeans and pullover, Harriet unearths a thin manila folder.

She hasn't the foggiest idea what the folder might possibly contain or what Caroline's job at Office Depot might look like on paper. The fact is, it's hard to imagine an Office Depot employee bringing their job home at all, let alone on vacation. What if it's not work-related at all? What if it's more legal difficulty or, worse, some medical concern Caroline is not telling her about? Hepatitis. Cancer. God knows, she abused her body over the years.

One eye on the bathroom door, Harriet peeks inside the folder.

Her immediate response is relief. No arrest warrants, no grim medical diagnosis, but real estate listings, several pages of them. Black-and-white photos, accompanied by a blur of vital statistics which Harriet can't make out without her reading glasses. Is Caroline buying a house? How can she afford it? Are the listings rentals? Not until she spots the familiar Jace Real Estate logo does Harriet's heart begin to race. Is Caroline moving to the peninsula? Impossible. Skip? Before Harriet can fetch her glasses, the shower sputters to a halt and the clashing metallic rings tinkle as Caroline pulls the curtain back. Harriet slaps the folder shut and replaces the jeans and sweater atop it, quickly busying herself with the dresser, as Caroline emerges, wrapped in a towel.

Watching Caroline dress, the thrilling realization skitters down Harriet's spine: her children are moving closer at last! For years, she's been trying to lure Skip to the peninsula. Mornings when the relentless rain is beating down on Seattle's north end, and the gloom crowds in from all corners, Harriet phones Skip to report the glorious blue skies awaiting him in the banana belt, a mere seventy miles to the west. You've said yourself, you can work from anywhere, she reminds him. No crime, no traffic. Did she mention she's out in her garden, right now, sipping an Arnold Palmer? She's even tried to entice Caroline to relocate, though with less frequency. Dear, there's nothing for you in the city, she tells her. They've got a Home Depot right here in Sequim.

Now it's actually happening!

No matter that they're doing it because they think their mother is helpless. No matter that they're likely to drive her crazy with their hounding and snooping or that they're liable to take away her car keys. They can have them as long as they're willing to chauffeur her around town according to her needs. The fact is, she'd welcome the opportunity not to drive. She's willing to give up some of her independence if it means her children will be closer. She can continue her healing with Caroline. Skip can clean those gutters this fall. The three of them can dine together on occasion. There's much to hope for. Of course, there will be disadvantages, small annoyances, occasional unpleasantness, but it's worth the trade-off just to have someone to bake for, someone to see a matinee with.

"So how was your thing at the pool, anyway?" says Caroline.

"Lovely," says Harriet. "Not too vigorous, you'll be glad to know. And how did your business go?"

"So far, so good," she says nonchalantly, slipping into her pullover.

"Well, that's exciting."

Caroline looks at her strangely. "Is it?"

"Why, of course it is. When were you going to tell me?"

"Tell you what exactly, Mom?"

"About the house."

"I was going to talk to you about it at dinner tonight," she says, sliding into her jeans.

"Who's actually going to live in the house, dear?"

"Whoever buys it, I guess. There's really no way of knowing, Mom."

"Well, I assume Skip's buying it. You can't afford it on your salary, can you?"

Caroline looks momentarily stricken as she lowers herself next to Harriet in the love seat. "Oh, Mom," she says pityingly. "No, you don't understand. Those are comps."

"Comps?"

"Comparably priced houses."

"Comparable to what? Are you getting your real estate license, dear? That's wonderful."

"No, Mom. These places are all priced comparably to yours. They're all three bedroom, two baths, on two to five acres that have sold in the past six months. They're all with fifteen miles of your house."

"I'm afraid I still don't understand."

"Dwight says the market is rebounding and that it may not last. In fact, he thinks the bottom may drop out again any day."

A cold hand seizes Harriet's heart. "Dwight?"

"Mom, just listen to reason, here."

Harriet's got a mind to stand up and walk out of the room. But she fears her knees will give out if she stands.

"You're sitting on nearly a half million dollars if you sell now. It's time to list it, Mom."

Stonily silent, Harriet turns her face to the veranda as this new, more sinister revelation settles in.

When Caroline sets a consoling hand on Harriet's knee, she brushes it off like a tarantula.

March 25, 2006
(HARRIET AT SIXTY-NINE)

Admit it, Harriet, deep down, you're just a little disappointed it's Caroline and not Skip coming to visit you on this glorious Saturday in early spring. And make no mistake, it is glorious. You could reach out and touch the mountains. The birds are atwitter, as they flit about your garden. You'll eat at the patio table, where already it's pushing seventy degrees.

Yet Caroline's imminent arrival troubles you. Too bad Mildred and Clark have canceled at the last minute—again. Too bad Bernard is not likely to move from his roost in front of the television all afternoon, where he cycles endlessly among collegiate football, PBS, and the History Channel.

Still, you're determined to give Caroline the benefit of the doubt and make this a nice visit. You prepare a roast, with new potatoes and carrots, and you bake a cake, lemon chiffon. You clean the kitchen and bathroom, you dust, you make up the guest room and arrange flowers, hellebore and bleeding hearts. Everything is perfect.

Ah, but it never is, is it, Harriet? Your daughter arrives with gin on her breath, prickly as a saguaro. Nails bitten to the quick.

Brunch conversation is one-sided: Caroline's litany of woes. Another lay-off. Another boss screwing her out of her unemployment benefit. At fifteen, Cassidy is threatening to move out of the house. She's dating a twenty-year-old thug with an ace-of-spades tattoo on his neck. The kid is practically living with them. She ought to start charging them rent. Really, she's harboring a runaway.

Of course you know what's coming. It always comes, trailing Caroline like a fog of gin. Before your wayward daughter can muster the nerve to be direct, you're already reaching for your checkbook, though not, of course, before Bernard has retreated to the television with his plate. Not because Bernard would disapprove (though he might) but because Caroline still somehow manages to be proud.

Seven hundred dollars. Last time it was eight. Six months ago, it was a thousand. And what does this money buy you? Not even peace of mind. Not even a phone call once a month. But you write the check, you always write the check. In the memo line you write "gift." She's your daughter, Harriet. You tell yourself that her problems are still your responsibility, even at thirty-eight. Who knew that one phone call from New Mexico all those years ago would mark the beginning of a long pattern, a legacy of trouble and expense, of bailouts and rescues and interventions?

It breaks your heart to watch her struggle. You want nothing more than happiness for your daughter. You'd do anything to make that happen. But today you finally draw the line, Harriet.

Hours after the check has been written, the plates have been cleared, and the conversation has (at times) even managed a certain level of ease, who do you find at the hallway desk, stealthily rummaging through your purse, rifling through your credit cards like a professional?

The thing that surprises you, now and later, is your calmness. Not so much as a vent of steam from Mount St. Harriet. One word, three letters is all, its meaning delivered with such clarity, such finality, such gravity, that it elicits no comeback or defense whatsoever.

Out. As in, O-U-T. As in, completely out—out of your house, out of your life, and as much as possible, out of your thoughts and prayers.

When Bernard ambles into the kitchen for a snack a half hour later and wonders what happened to Caroline, you give him the skinny. He nods. As always, he shares your prejudice. You can't help but wonder if he knows the truth.

It will be nearly four years, and seven steps, before you hear from Caroline again, when she calls you on Easter morning to make her amends.

August 22, 2015
(HARRIET AT SEVENTY-EIGHT)

The Crow's Nest is almost tasteful, with its burgundy club chairs and panoramic views. The light is subdued, but cheerful, the temperature perfect, the chatter so polite as to be but a pleasant murmur beneath a tinkling of silver and glassware. Tonight Harriet's club soda tastes colder.

On a stool before the gaslit hearth, a handsome young man with a thick, lustrous head of hair and Scottish brogue (or maybe Irish), strums an acoustic guitar to the tune of "Danny Boy."

Under the circumstances, Harriet is finding it hard to maintain her anger. It's possible, she's forced to admit, that Caroline actually has her best interest in mind. Viewing her life from some distance, Harriet can see how her situation might look to her daughter: osteoarthritis, dented side panels, phantom WD-40 cans. All that house, all that yard, all those stairs. And there she is, pushing eighty years old, brittle-boned and stooped, two hours from her nearest relative. Yes, from this vantage, Harriet can see why there might be legitimate cause for concern. And for the first time, she's touched by her daughter's solicitude. Tonight Harriet is willing, once again, to give Caroline the benefit of the doubt. She's earned it.

"Just have a glass of wine, Mom. Don't worry about me."

"No, dear, I'm fine."

But a glass of wine sounds awfully good.

"Seriously, Mom. Just enjoy yourself. I'm around booze all the time."

"Fine, then. I'll order a glass."

Harriet's glad Caroline talked her into it. The sweet white wine is a perfect accent to the velveteen air of the Crow's Nest, a perfect complement to the sad, sweet longing of "Cockles and Mussels." What's more, Caroline seems perfectly comfortable with it. In fact, between sets, she flags the passing waitress and orders Harriet another glass, which is quite thoughtful if not a little surprising, all things considered, though Harriet has a sneaking suspicion she knows who will be picking up the tab. But what's a few dollars, next to peace and tranquillity with her daughter?

Having conceded her campaign, as far as Harriet can tell, Caroline makes no further mention of the house. They do what they never seem to be able to do: they while away the evening with agreeable conversation, treading the past lightly, avoiding points of contention, keeping the reins on their sarcasm.

"Oh, these old songs are so romantic, aren't they?" says Harriet.

"They are," says Caroline. "I've have to admit. I'm a sucker for an Irish accent."

"Oh, look," chimes Harriet. "It's Kurt!"

Indeed, Kurt ambles in wearing a gray T-shirt (with sleeves!) that says LOOK, DON'T TOUCH. He's clean-shaven, and his hair's in order. Harriet gives him a little wave, but Kurt doesn't register it, as he takes a stool at the bar, his back pointed squarely at Harriet and Caroline.

"Shall I invite him to join us?"

"Mom, please, no."

"Whatever you say."

"Thanks, Mom."

"I wasn't going to try and set you up, you know?"

"I know. I'd rather it just be the two of us tonight, though." Harriet pats her on the knee. "That's sweet, dear."

"And Mom, I'm sorry I discouraged you from coming on this cruise. Seriously. I underestimated you."

"You meant well, dear, I know that. It's also possible that you overestimated the cruise."

"A little of both, I guess. Anyway, I'm glad you didn't listen to me. Are you having fun?"

"Oh yes, dear," says Harriet with a slug of wine.

"Do you want another glass or anything?"

"I've had plenty. Gracious, if I drank another, you'd have to carry me out of here. How about you, dear? Another club soda?"

"What's the use, I can't feel it."

"Squawk. That's what she said," quips Harriet.

Caroline grins. "Well played, Mom."

"Why—*hic*—thank you," says Harriet.

"Look, Mom," says Caroline, reaching into her purse. "We need to resolve some stuff."

Harriet straightens up in her chair and summons what concern she can muster. "What is it, dear?"

"Your future," says Caroline. "We can't ignore it." She sets some forms on the table and returns to her purse for a pen. "It's just stuff designed to make things easier for you. Mostly, it's a precaution."

Suddenly, Harriet is alert. The warmth drains from her in a flash. "What is this?" She snatches up the paper and dons her glasses.

"It's in case anything happens," says Caroline. "And you're unable to make a decision or whatever."

It doesn't take long for Harriet to recognize the significance of the paper. "You don't actually expect me to sign this, do you?"

"Mom, it's just in case."

"Is that why you've been trying to get me drunk, Caroline? You actually think you can dupe me into signing away my freedom?"

Harriet stands up too fast and nearly loses her balance.

"Mom, sit down. Let me explain."

"You'd sell my house right out from under me, wouldn't you? Lock me away and help yourself to my bank account."

"Sit down, Mom, you're making a scene."

Indeed, neighboring tables have begun to take notice.

But Harriet doesn't care. "On top of everything else, you bungled it, Caroline. Even if you did dupe me into signing this, you'd need two witnesses. My God, you could have picked a shrewder conspirator than Dwight Honeycutt!"

The music stops. At the bar, Kurt has turned to see what the commotion is.

"Mom, sit down, please," says Caroline. Rising to her feet, she coaxes Harriet back into her chair. Harriet complies but only because she feels woozy.

July 1, 1966
(HARRIET AT TWENTY-NINE)

Look at you, Harriet Chance, so diligent, so fastidious in your attention to detail! It's Friday at 6 p.m., and most of the office left hours ago for the holiday. But not you, Harriet. There are documents to file, motions to draft, letters to write. A pile of work that would daunt most people but not Ms. Harriet Chance. The productivity thrills you. Every day you learn something new about the vast quagmire of law, and bit by bit you see the big picture coming together like a jigsaw puzzle.

When you're really in a good groove, you allow yourself to daydream, don't you? With your enthusiasm and your sterling work ethic, is it so impossible to believe that you could go back to school and earn a law degree? Isn't that what your father had planned for you? Isn't the timing right? You've got your days, with Skip at school. You could keep your job and go to school nights. You could pay for child care with your own income. You could still be your idealized self: independent, decisive, outspoken.

Ah, but you're just musing, aren't you Harriet? You wouldn't dare share this dream with anyone, least of all your husband, who still seems slightly amused by your professional endeavors, though he is supportive. But what on earth would he say when you tell him you want to be a lawyer?

There is one person upon whom your good, hard work is apparently not lost, one person who has professed to believe in you all along, who has encouraged you, a person with whom you've always shared a unique, if not always healthy, repartee as confidants. And he just so happens to be the only one left in the office.

Listen to Charlie Fitzsimmons commend you on your superlative work. Telling you he can count on you one hundred percent, that he trusts your work and your character implicitly, that nobody is quite as quick and efficient, and discreet. Charlie's not as old-fashioned as some. He believes the right woman can do most anything a man can do. In fact, he can see increasing the right woman's responsibilities, expanding her sphere of influence. Who knows, maybe even subsidizing her continued education—his words, not yours.

At first, your shoulders tighten beneath his touch, which stirs an old confusion and a racing heart. But his words embolden you. The fact that until five minutes ago the man was repellent to you only seems to inflame you more, as though you've actually managed to turn the emotion inside out, unleashing a reckless impulse you could never have guessed at.

No, it's not Charlie's empty promises of mobility that set your heart to racing, nor the fact that his words echo your daydreams. In fact, it has little to do with your ambition. It's something else. Three things, actually: One, an almost instinctive obedience to authority, which you abhor in yourself, though you have no power to stop it. Two, some dark impetus beyond reason, some grotesque thing that's been living under a rock your whole life (let's call it repression). And lastly, there's the truth, plain and shabby as a hobo's trousers, that you believe yourself to be worthless, though you don't fully know it yet, at least you haven't formally acknowledged it.

This is your life, Harriet, taking a hairpin turn.

Take a good long look, before we move on, like a rubbernecker at the sight of a collision. Unthinkable as it is, that's really you, Harriet Chance, black-and-white-checked skirt hiked six inches above the waist, bare legs splayed on the mahogany desktop, as Charlie Fitzsimmons, pants bunched around his ankles, toupee listing badly to one side, empties himself inside of you.

Welcome to the sexual revolution, Harriet Chance! You won't be staying long.

August 22, 2015
(HARRIET AT SEVENTY-EIGHT)

As soon as the dizziness subsides, Harriet gulps the last of her wine and sets the empty glass on top of the documents. A little wine drips down her chin, but she makes no effort to wipe it off, leaving it there like a challenge. Suppressing a hiccup, she stares Caroline down from across the table until Caroline is forced to avert her eyes.

Harriet promptly flags the waitress and orders another glass.

"I thought you said you've had enough."

"Mind your own business."

Caroline is polishing her monkey's fist under the table, as though she might conjure a spell out of the thing.

Harriet's temples pound with rage. The camaraderie, the healing, the easy laughter—all just a ruse.

"Durable power of attorney? Why not legal guardianship, Caroline? I'm sure they've got a notary on board. Then you could really have your way with my assets. Lock me up in Sherwood Arms and throw away the key, why don't you?"

"Nobody's trying to lock you up. And Sunny Acres is hardly Sherwood Arms."

"My God, you could've just asked for money. It always worked before."

"I don't want your money. But now that you mention it, you might have left me a little something after Dad died."

"Funny, I had other things on my mind, Caroline. But you're right," she says bitterly. "You're absolutely right."

She fishes her checkbook from her purse and picks up Caroline's pen and quickly scrawls out a check, barely legible, for eight thousand dollars. She writes nothing in the memo line.

"C'mon, Mom, knock it off."

"Should I add a zero? Would you rather I leave the amount blank?" Harriet tears the check from her register and pushes it across the table. "There, are you happy? Don't cash it until we get back. I'll have to transfer the funds."

Caroline pushes the check back.

Harriet volleys the check back, then picks up the pen again. "And while I'm at it."

She grabs the document and flips to the second page and signs it, hand trembling. "There," she says, to the bewildered couple at the adjacent table. "You saw that." Then, turning back to Caroline: "You'll need signatures."

Harriet stands up, just as her glass of wine arrives. "And for the record, your father is still alive."

"See? It's statements like that that make me think you're—"

"That's not what I mean, Caroline."

"What are you talking about?"

Harriet looks her daughter straight in the eye, unflinchingly. "All these years you've been begrudging the wrong man."

Caroline leaves off rubbing her knot, matching Harriet's gaze for what feels like forty-eight years.

This time it's Harriet who looks away first. "Now look what you've made me do," she says, and walks away from the table, wobbling slightly. As she exits the Crow's Nest, a wave of remorse courses through her like nausea. She pauses briefly to look back at her daughter, pale and perplexed, fondling her monkey's fist again. And in that moment realizes she just made the biggest mistake of her life.

July 1, 1966
(HARRIET AT TWENTY-NINE)

Okay, maybe the second biggest mistake of your life. You're wracked with guilt the instant Charlie Fitzsimmons climbs off of you, mops the sweat off his brow, and straightens his toupee. You maintain silence as you dress, an easy state of affairs for the two of you, let's face it.

Before you can begin to unravel the mess you've made, before you can begin to calculate your next move, you feel it. A tickle at first. Something takes root in you in that instant, even as Charlie pulls his pants up and fastens his belt. Yes, something starts growing, something that will still be with you forty-nine years later, Harriet, something you'll never be able to outrun: contempt. Mostly for yourself but, to a lesser degree, contempt for the world. And yes, Harriet, as tough as it is to admit, as awful as it sounds, contempt for the unwitting life that has taken root inside you.

Now let's be perfectly clear on something: You want to get rid of this, this . . . what shall we call it, child? That seems a little premature. This thing? That's a little objectifying, don't you think?

Hell, why mince words? Let's just call it Caroline.

The second-to-last thing in the world you need right now is another child (the last thing being an illegitimate one). But you really have no choice, Harriet, at least not a safe or reputable or affordable one—and many would say not a moral one. It's 1966. The National Organization for Women is less than a week old. Legal abortion is still four years off, a reality so distant that Margaret Sanger won't live to see it. The available options are all prohibitive one way or another. They involve back alleys or intercontinental flights or precarious home remedies. Your only legitimate (sorry, poor word choice) option may be a trip to the roller skating rink, where a couple of good hard falls might do the trick.

So you've got that going for you.

Sick with worry and wracked with guilt, but certain beyond all reasonable doubt that you are pregnant, you return home late from work that evening and find that Bernard has prepared himself beans and toast and sits in his chair working a crossword. You graze his shoulder on the way past. He tries to pat your fanny. Playfully, you elude him. But inside you're dying. Stealing to the bathroom, you take a shower so hot it burns, scrubbing yourself raw to rid yourself of Charlie Fitzsimmons, inside and out. Your efforts, of course, are futile.

Your life has jumped the tracks, Harriet Chance. So what's a grown girl to do?

In bed that night, under the covers, though your stomach and your heart are in knots, and the very idea is revolting in every aspect, you take Bernard firmly in your hand until he's at full attention, then you straddle him in the darkness, hating yourself, sobbing so quietly he can't hear you, hoping beyond hope that he can somehow unroot or dislodge your error, your—dare we say it—mistake. Not to be crass, but the plain truth is, when he rolls you over on your back to assume missionary, you're wishing Bernard could fuck the life out of you.

Not really his style. After three minutes, or an hour, or a year, Bernard groans his release and rolls off of you, whereupon he promptly falls asleep without a care in the world.

From here on out, Harriet, it's all a charade. Thank heavens, Charlie Fitzsimmons was a Caucasian, or this one would come back in nine months to bite you, for sure. Maybe not an ideal solution to your problem (and your problem is just getting started here), but hey, given the available choices, what was a girl to do?

Observe, Harriet, the world's biggest Band-Aid. Believe it or not, it'll get the job done for almost fifty years. But man, is it gonna sting when you pull that baby off.

August 22, 2015
(HARRIET AT SEVENTY-EIGHT)

The frigid air of the observation deck sobers Harriet almost immediately as she leans on the rail, staring dumbly at the blackened form of the mountains, crouching in the moonless night. Somewhere out in the vast, dim quiet, there's an answer for everything. But all Harriet can hear is the wind rocketing past her ears. All she can feel is dread, cold and implacable as the Yukon night.

Rising at the back of her throat is a clot of emotion, crude and shapeless as a lump of coal.

Dear God, help me see clearly. Give me the strength, give me the courage.

But praying doesn't help. This one's not in God's hands.

This one stands squarely on Harriet's shoulders. And not the other Harriet.

Caroline's not in the room when Harriet returns. She sheds her jacket and moves restlessly about the cabin for a few minutes, finally taking up the remote. Flipping through channels, she pauses the instant she sees black and white. Good old black and white, so soothing next to the barrage of color.

There's Bogey on the screen with Bacall. *Key Largo,* an old favorite. A movie she'd seen for the first time ten years after its original release, a second screening with Bernard at the Uptown Theater, before the new owners gutted the place. They'd sat on the balcony, Harriet pregnant with Skip, though nobody knew it yet.

Nineteen fifty-eight. It doesn't seem possible.

Suddenly she feels Bernard's presence.

"She's got my feet in case you hadn't noticed."

He's beside her on the love seat, his voice cracked and wafer thin, only a wisp of ghostly white hair left atop his spotted crown.

"You knew it all along, didn't you?"

"Like you knew about Mildred? No, Harriet, I suppose both of us were more than a bit nearsighted. It happens."

They fall silent, turning their attention to the screen, where the shutters are banging and pictures are falling off the wall, and Edward G. Robinson's bug-eyed agitation is reaching its crescendo.

"You ought to apologize."

"I'm sorry, Bernard."

"I mean to her."

Harriet sighs, muting the television. "God, what a mess I've made."

"You had some help along the way."

"How can I ever undo it?"

"Technically, you can't. But you can start over. Or try."

"What if it's too late?"

"There's always that possibility. But don't let it stop you from trying. Believe me, you'll regret it, Harriet. Just look at me."

"You're right," she says, standing. She gathers her purse and coat, leaving Bernard on the love seat.

"I assume you won't be here when I get back?"

"Probably not," he says. "I'm what you might call AWOL."

"Will you come back?"

"Yes."

"You promise."

"I promise. Now go," he says, shooing her toward the door. "And turn the volume up on your way out, would you? This is the best part."

"Bernard."

"What?" he says.

"I suppose I should thank you."

Disembarking the elevator, Harriet is determined to make the necessary revisions, whatever they may be. She hasn't the foggiest idea what she's going to say to her daughter to smooth over a lifetime of deceit, no clue what apology or explanation could possibly inspire forgiveness for forty-eight years of misgivings, but Harriet marches down the corridor with purpose.

By the time she arrives at the Crow's Nest, the crowd has thinned out. Caroline has vacated the table. Harriet's heart sinks. She could be anywhere. Scanning the room, Harriet spots Kurt, still hunched at the bar, nursing a green bottle of beer.

"Dear, you didn't happen see where my daughter disappeared to, did you?"

No sooner has she said it than she sees it on the bar top near to Kurt, next to an empty highball, rope worn smooth as wax: Caroline's monkey's fist.

As if on cue, Caroline saunters back from the restroom, sneering the instant she registers Harriet. She's drunk, it's obvious.

C TO Charmichael is dressed for business today. Crisply pleated dark slacks, starched shirt, obedient hair. Even his bald spot looks shiny. He circles the desk upon Bernard's entrance, and perches on the front edge, folding his arms like a disappointed boss.

"It appears, Candidate Chance, you've been up to something. Clearly, you've not been spending your time contemplating nothing, or you wouldn't be back in my office. That's two strikes, you understand. One more than the guidelines allow for."

Instinctively, Bernard bows his head and casts his eyes toward his shoe tops.

"Frankly, I'm at a loss, Chance. Your military record indicates no history of insubordination. Your taxes were all in order. Your home life was a mess, but that's not so uncommon. Your attendance was exemplary, outside the confines of husbandry and fatherhood, that is. I really didn't see you as a flight risk."

"I'm not running, sir. I'm just trying to help."

"Help whom? It would appear that you're trying to improve your own case. Trying to get your wife to forgive you so you can neutralize your guilt. You're not the first, you know? And neither are you the shrewdest nor the most worthy, not by a long shot. Let's see, so far, you've defended your mistress, displaced some WD-40, eaten some corned beef, and watched Humphrey Bogart. I'd say you're not staging much of a defense. So as your chief supervisor, let me offer you a little advice. Make yourself comfortable, Candidate. There's plenty of improvements we can make right here. We could work on that impulse control, clean up your language, focus on a few blind spots. With a little diligence and some elbow grease, you could make CTO in five years if you walk a straight line. You could at least make deputy. Don't blow it, Chance. Whatever you think you're doing, it's not worth it. Accept your remorse, and put it in a box. Compartmentalize, for heaven's sake. This isn't permanent. It doesn't have to be. There's still a chance for you. You didn't reveal anything about the nature of transition, right? Nothing about the steps? Nothing about the eight principles. You've simply meddled in your former life, so what? A little interference. It happens more frequently than you might think, actually. That's why I'm here. To make corrections. I'm not going to lie to you, this is a strike against you, sure, but it's by no means insurmountable. Save yourself, Chance."

"Sir, with all due respect, this is not about me anymore. This is about them. I can't undo the damage, that's perfectly clear, but I can sweep up some of the rubble I left behind, and I can get out of their way for good."

"Don't do it, Candidate. You won't even have a chance to regret it. Remember the nothing. Always remember the nothing."

"I gotta say good-bye. Please, sir, you gotta grant me this. I promised her. She's expecting me."

"I admire your commitment, Chance, I do. But it's a little late in the game. I'm not gonna look the other way this time. I'm afraid leniency is simply out of the question. If you go back, you'll be sealing your fate. I'll have no choice but to send someone after you."

"I understand, sir. You've got your orders."

"I'm not sure you do, Chance. Just to be clear, you'll be choosing nothing. Nothing at all. As in, end of story. You'll be wishing for test patterns, a hum—anything at all. Only you won't know it, Chance."

"Yessir."

CTO Charmichael shakes his head grimly. "You're making a mistake."

"Maybe so, sir."

"You can't hide. They'll find you. Sooner or later, they'll nab you. And when they do . . ."

"Yessir, end of story."

March 13, 2003
(HARRIET AT SIXTY-SIX)

You never saw Caroline as the nurturing type. Naturally, you are circumspect when she tells you that twelve-year-old Cassidy is like the daughter she never had. Rail thin Cassidy, with her stiff upper lip, and those deep-set, sullen eyes, so far beyond their years. Really, what Caroline has come to tell you is that she needs to borrow a thousand dollars.

This business with the runaway Cassidy will not end well, you tell yourself, as ever, writing another check. And piece by piece, the evidence will support your case, as Caroline fails in her role as mentor, fails to set a good example for Cassidy, and fails miserably as an authority figure.

But here we are again, getting ahead of ourselves.

Maybe, Harriet, you were wrong about Caroline's capacity

to nurture. Maybe you just didn't know where to look all those years. Maybe Caroline was right when she said you never gave her enough credit.

Exhibit A: Remember the white rat? That revolting little red-eyed rodent that went everywhere with her, sophomore year of high school? Crawling up and down her sleeves, lolling around in her pockets, nibbling at her earlobes. You know, the one that got loose in the house, the one that scurried right past your feet when you were making Bernard's toast, the one that came to an abrupt stop when you brained it with a skillet. To be fair, the damn thing startled you, a white blur—it could have been anything. And you were only trying to divert its course. A lucky shot, really.

That rat had a name, Harriet, it was Mr. Obidiah Whiskers. And when you crushed Obidiah Whiskers, with one cast-iron stroke, you crushed Caroline, too. Yes, that sounds silly—it did then, and it still does. I mean, c'mon, it was a rat! You even offered to buy her a new one. And while nobody expected you to shed a tear for the unfortunate Mr. Whiskers, you might have showed a little more compassion than "It's only a rat, Caroline."

She was just a kid, Harriet. Worse, a teenager. A little empathy might have been nice. An apology of some sort. Just sayin'.

And let's talk about the mutt, while we're at it, the one Caroline brought home on her sixteenth birthday, the little brown one missing half an ear, and the ferocious breath, and the cataract clouding its right eye. That was Boogaloo, in case you've forgotten, and Caroline was obviously smitten beyond hope with the pathetic creature. The fact is, she could have used a companion about then. Better than the delinquents she was running around with.

But you wouldn't give in, would you, Harriet? You wouldn't even let her ask her father before you made her drop off the dog at the humane society. Was it really the new wood floors? Was it really your allergies? Was it really fair to speak on Bernard's behalf?

You didn't want your daughter to have a dog.

Gads, Harriet, even *your* mother let you have a dog! So why would you deny your daughter a dog? She would have made any concession to keep that dog. She promised to pay for its upkeep. The miserable thing might have happily slept in the garage. Probably Caroline would've slept in the garage with it.

Admit it, you were just being cheap with your daughter. It was a learned behavior, not that that's an any kind of excuse.

Rats, dogs, foundling children, there's a pattern here, Harriet, though it's taken you nearly a half century to acknowledge it. Maybe your daughter's not perfect, maybe she can't tell her own story the way she'd like to. Maybe something is stopping her.

September 9, 1986
(HARRIET AT FORTY-NINE)

For nineteen years you've been looking at your daughter's horsey features and wiry hair, and biting your tongue, thinking of Charlie Fitzsimmons and wondering if Bernard has ever intuited the fact that he's raising somebody else's daughter. But when you pick her up at the bus station upon her return from New Mexico, having wired her the money for the ticket three days prior (unbeknownst to Bernard), it's not Charlie Fitzsimmons you see in your daughter's bewildered young face, but yourself, Harriet.

Immediately you notice a change about her. Her eyes reflect experiences you do not recognize, and some that you do. You will not judge her, not this time. How could you? You don't say a word about the tattoo on the ride to the clinic. You don't ask about the job she held for six months in Albuquerque, or the winds that blew her there in the first place. You're hardly listening, as she tells you about her stints in Santa Maria or Tucson. You don't so much as inquire about the father of her unborn child or whether this is the first time such a thing has happened. There are many things you do not want to know.

What's important, here, is that this thing go no further. This thing stops right here, and Caroline goes on with her life. Because there *is* a choice, a simple choice, one you never had. The fact is, you're trying to save your daughter. You won't even allow her to discuss or consider the other options, not if she wants to live under your roof. And really, where else can she go, Harriet, that she hasn't already been in the past year? A shelter? Back on the street?

Make no mistake: your intentions are good. So don't judge yourself too harshly.

Everything will turn out right, you tell your daughter. Just be grateful there's a solution, dear. Consider yourself lucky you have a choice. You can put this behind you. You can still live the life you want to live. And don't worry, your father doesn't have to know a thing, dear. This is just between us.

This pact between you is the last secret you and Caroline will share for twenty-nine years, during which time both of you will withhold some doozies.

The Caroline who greets you in the waiting room a few hours after the procedure looks five years younger than the one that went in. Yes, much too young to be a mother, you think. Look what she's saved herself from. Look at the opportunities still available to her without a child weighing her down. You made the right decision, Harriet, whether or not it was yours to make.

On the drive home from the clinic, Caroline cries softly in the passenger's seat, face turned to the side window. You do your best to comfort her. You reassure her. You resist the temptation to lecture her on the subject of birth control, an option you never exercised yourself. You do not, however, solicit discussion or invite second-guessing where the matter of choice is concerned. Pulling the sleeve of Caroline's blouse down over her tattoo, you pat her encouragingly on the knee.

There, there, you say, don't cry. A fresh start, dear. You'll see.

But that fresh start will look more like a spiral, won't it, Harriet? Things will only get worse for Caroline. In six months, she'll be out on the street again, looking for a family.

You see, Harriet, something else died along with that unborn child: an opportunity. What your daughter never told you, Harriet, what you wouldn't have heard, anyway, is that she wanted to keep it.

August 22, 2015
(HARRIET AT SEVENTY-EIGHT)

Caroline stops just short of the bar and, donning a curdled grin, reaches into her pocket.

"Good," she says. "I'm glad you're back, Mom."

She pulls out the check and rips it in half, then tears it in half again, and watches the pieces flutter to the floor, before resuming her stool next to Kurt.

"And just so you know, Mom, just so there's no misunderstanding, it's Skip, okay? He wants your money, not me. I'm just his stooge."

Stunned, Harriet reaches out and grasps the bar for support.

"That's right, Mom. Golden boy Skipper, your *little man*, he's losing his house. And you're the solution to all his problems. Me, I just get a free vacation and some new duds."

"Well, how did he afford to send you money?"

"He forged a check. Yep, one of yours. Turns out I'm not the only criminal you raised."

"Where did he get my checkbook?"

"From me, of course."

Harriet stands there, dumb as a side of beef. But before the repercussions can settle in, before she can react to this news, she reminds herself why she's here and shakes off the blow.

"Caroline, honey, you don't want to do this. C'mon, dear, come with me. Let's get some air and straighten all this out."

Just as she says it, the barkeep delivers Caroline a fresh drink, which she clutches immediately.

Harriet shoots Kurt a withering look.

Kurt shrugs helplessly.

"Oh, give him a break, Mom. You're the one trying to set me up with him." Caroline slugs down half the drink in a single toss.

"Maybe she's right," says Kurt. "Maybe y'all ought to have that talk, Caroline."

Caroline slams the highball glass down with gusto. "Fine," she says, pushing off of the bar, her stool tipping backward, as she stands. "Let's have a little talk."

Behind her, Kurt pantomimes an elaborate apology. How could he know?

Harriet leads Caroline out by the elbow, though halfway down the corridor Caroline wrests her elbow free and steps up her pace, arriving at the elevator well in advance of Harriet, where she pushes the call button and shifts her weight impatiently from one foot to the other. Harriet knows better than to breach the silence at this point. Having been there herself so many times, she knows that any appeal to Caroline whatsoever at this moment, anything besides a strict observance of silence over the next minute or two, will only result in escalation.

But something happens to Caroline in the close quarters of the elevator: all the defiance seems to drain out of her, right before Harriet's eyes. Every muscle of her body seems to slacken at once.

"Thanks for getting me out of there," she says.

Harriet reaches out and clutches her daughter's hand, but Caroline pulls away as the elevator eases to a stop.

In the blustery air of the observation deck, Caroline, her kinky hair blowing sideways, crosses her arms over her chest.

"Dear, maybe we should go fetch your coat," says Harriet.

"No."

"But darling, you'll freeze."

"I want to freeze."

The deck is deserted, as they drift wordlessly toward the stern, with the wind at their backs.

"Well, I don't know how you can stand it," says Harriet.

At midship, a steady blast from the heating vents envelops them suddenly in the illusion of a tropical night.

"Now that's more like it," says Harriet, lowering herself onto a wide bench. "Sit down, dear."

But Caroline moves to the rail, where she stares into the darkness. Harriet wonders whether she should go to the rail or stay put and give Caroline her space. Watching her daughter's back, the slow rhythmic convulsing of her shoulders, her dark mess of hair blowing crazily, Harriet contemplates the distance between them and wishes with an ache that the gap was only the mere ten or twelve feet now separating them. If only she could will her daughter back through the years.

Harriet is about to go to her when Caroline turns. "Five years thirty-one days," she says, plopping down next to Harriet. "Fuck. Fuck. Fuck."

"It's my fault, dear."

"I've been looking for an excuse. You and Skip just made it convenient for me."

"Oh, Caroline. I'm so sorry. I'm a wicked person."

"What are we even talking about, here, Mom? Who am I? Who should I be begrudging?"

Harriet balls her fists in her lap. She doesn't know where to begin. She supposes, with the vague personal dissatisfaction and the ancient self-loathing, for which Charlie Fitzsimmons was only an antidote, or perhaps a symptom of or, at most, only part of the cause. But where did that begin? And what was it? And how, at nearly eighty years old, could she not know this about herself?

"You know what?" says Caroline. "Maybe I don't wanna know. To tell you the truth, that might be too much right now."

She bows her head, her ragged breath giving way to a sob. "Goddamnit, I fucked up again. Why do I always fuck up? I swear to God, it's like I wanna fail. Skip's right."

"Forget Skip," says Harriet. "Don't talk like that. Part of it is genetic, you know. At least you've had the courage to face it. My God, Caroline, what did I ever do? And that may be the least of my problems. Lately, I'm discovering all kinds of deficits in myself. I don't even know who I am anymore, Caroline."

"Pfff. You're telling me. I never have, Mom, not my whole life."

"You'd think the growing pains would end at some point, or at least slow down," says Harriet. "But oh no."

"If anything, they accelerate," Caroline says.

Harriet scoots closer and tentatively takes her daughter's hand. This time, she accepts it.

"I'm sorry, dear. I've been a terrible mother. You did nothing to deserve me."

"Who is he?" she asks.

"His name is—was—Charlie Fitzsimmons."

"He's dead?"

"He must be."

"You loved him?"

"Never."

"Does he know about me?"

"No."

"Did Dad know?"

"No."

"So, I was . . . what, then? A mistake?"

"Don't ever say that."

"Well? Then what?"

And so, Harriet breathes deeply of the warm air, bows her head, falters once, falters twice, gives pause, and finally begins her explanation. It begins in the waning minutes of 1936, with a little girl, confetti in her hair, hanging upside down in a bassinet.

August 17, 1946
(HARRIET AT NINE)

Ding-dong-ding, thwack-thwack-thwack, how on earth did we arrive way back here, Harriet? It's 1946, and Vaughn Monroe is on the radio. If you listen closely, you can still hear them celebrating victory in Times Square.

Welcome to postwar America, where spirits are high. It's been another prosperous year in the Nathan household, and nobody throws a company barbecue like the boys at Nathan, Montgomery, Ferris, and Fitzsimmons. We're talking Indian smoked salmon. Waldorf salad. Frankfurters the size of Chiquita bananas. All the Coca-Cola a nine-year-old girl can drink.

And lucky you, Harriet, of all the youngsters, you get a ride on Charlie Fitzsimmons' speedboat, and boy, she's a beaut. Good old Charlie Fitzsimmons. The whiz kid is now a wizened veteran of the law. One of the best in the city. A silver-tongued fox, a real asset to the firm. Your father venerates the man, talks about him like the son he never had, though Charlie's only ten years younger.

But you don't like Charlie, do you, Harriet? Or maybe that's not entirely accurate. You are acutely ambiguous about Charlie.

On the drive home, in the backseat of your father's Hudson Commodore, top down, you finally muster the courage to say so.

"What do you mean you don't like the way he talks to you?" says your father, slightly tipsy—slightly, that is, by Nathan, Montgomery, Ferris, and Fitzsimmons standards.

"Like I'm already grown up," you say.

"Well, that's because you're a smart little girl," he says, his eyes smiling in the rear view mirror. "He respects you."

"Goodness," says your mother. "I hope you weren't rude. If you said anything impolite, young lady, we're driving right back to Charlie's this instant, and you're going to apologize."

"No," you say. "I promise I wasn't rude."

The thought of seeing Uncle Charlie (as he insists you call him) again, his coarse hands, his hairy knuckles, his gap-toothed smile, fills you with dread and anxiety. And the worst part is, you're ashamed for feeling thus, because Charlie thinks you're smart. Charlie respects you. Apparently, he's among the first. Charlie doesn't think you're fat. He forever goes out of his way to tell you how special you are.

"Well, then," says your mother, as though she can hear

your thoughts. "Maybe you ought to work on being a little more grateful."

"Yes, ma'am," you say.

Obviously, there's no use telling your parents why else you don't like Charlie Fitzsimmons, and his thin lips pressed against your forehead, and his hairy fingers groping beneath your bathing suit to pet you there. No use in telling them about the gentle way he spoke to you as he fondled you where your breasts had yet to begin their miraculous budding, nor the adoring things he said with his face buried in your lap. They wouldn't believe you anyway. There's no use telling anybody. Even Ginger, your golden retriever, doesn't seem to want to hear it. That will be your little secret for the next seventy years, Harriet. Just you and Uncle Charlie.

Charlie will continue to treat you with respect. He'll always make a point of telling you how smart and capable you are. How he could see right from the beginning how special you were, how he knew he could always trust you. Like your parents, he will regale you with the story of the upside-down baby girl. He'll tell you these things your whole life, right up to that after-hours dalliance on your office desk, twenty years hence, by which time, his speedboat will be a distant memory, buried deeply.

This is your life, Harriet, the one you didn't choose.

August 17, 1946
(HARRIET AT NINE)

N ow, now, not so fast, Harriet. We've still got business on Charlie's boat. Isn't it about time we revisit the scene of the . . . what shall we call it? The crime? That's what the proper authorities would call it—the proper authorities not being your parents, of course. How about "the event"? "Event" makes it sound singular. Though it was not singular, was it, Harriet? It was multiple. Serial might be a better word choice. But let's not quibble.

Let's just call it "the First Time."

It's summer, but out here on the open water, the wind cuts right through your chubby limbs. You've got goose flesh. The chill is thrilling. Charlie guns the engine, skittering over the chop, the boat leaping dolphinlike out of the water, the hull thrashing against the surface upon its rejoinder.

Look at you, Harriet, wide-eyed and grinning as your rump bounces up and down, half a foot off the padded berth, the horizon jumping right along with it. And Charlie is grinning, too, nay, Charlie is smiling like a madman. You can practically hear the wind whistling though his teeth.

It's not until Uncle Charlie stops the boat and leaves it to bob on the water like a cork that the chill is discomforting. The fact that he stopped the boat at all is discomforting in its own right. The craft is, after all, built for speed.

When Charlie sees you start to shiver, he comes to you, surefooted across the slippery deck of the bobbing boat and helps you out of your wet life preserver. Deftly, he begins to unclasp the—

Okay, fine, objection withheld. No need to dwell on the odious details, not for our purpose. This isn't hypnotherapy, Harriet, this is your life, an unsentimental accounting of it. You get to be judge, jury, and arbiter. You get to decide what's admissible. So strike the stuff about the offending fingers, the coarse stubble against your face, the whispered assurances. For the record, let's just say that once Charlie unfastens the straps, your life preserver, like your parents, ceases to protect you. And you, Harriet, you cease protecting yourself.

Yes, you were only nine years old, and no, it wasn't consensual, not by the letter of the law, anyway. Well, not by any letter, actually. But still, let's talk about your complicity in the affair. You could have resisted. Sure, you were in open water with no one around for a half mile. Still, you might have put up some kind of fuss. Sound travels a long ways across water. Surely, you must have learned that somewhere along the line by third grade. Think about it: Charlie was never about brute force, not in the courtroom or anywhere else. Charlie was about finesse, remember? Persuasion. He never threatened you. Quite the contrary. You had an unspoken understanding all those years.

Not to let Charlie off of the hook, but in hindsight, a little kicking and screaming might have saved you some trouble. Any kind of resistance at all might've done the trick. Even a simple no would have bought you some time. Rest assured, the other you would have put up a fight.

But you always were a quiet child, Harriet. Too quiet. And let's face it, Charlie wasn't used to taking no for an answer.

Now that we're getting right down to the nitty-gritty, let's give voice, at long last, to that unspoken understanding you shared with Uncle Charlie, from the First Time, to hallway gropings, to the office desk.

If you can name it, Harriet, maybe you can tame it.

You owed Charlie Fitzsimmons, didn't you? You owed him your life. And he took it from you, didn't he? It all began on that motorboat, that's when you started paying, that's where your path diverged from the other you. Bit by bit, he stole your confidence, little by little, he widened the gap between you and the you you might have become. He took your newly developed voice and stripped you of the power to tell your own story. He exacted his debt in self-esteem. You paid silently in shame, Harriet, in unfulfilled potential, in unexplored possibility. And you're still paying, all these years later.

And somehow, in spite of it all, Charlie Fitzsimmons never lost your respect, exercising that same finesse and expert persuasion that made him such a formidable opponent in the courtroom and such a hero at the dinner table. You can't fault yourself for being bested by the best, Harriet. You weren't even in fourth grade.

It ought to seem obvious. Lordy, it ought to go without saying, but somehow, some way, inconceivably, through the warped lens of your wounded self-image, the verdict has been lost on you all these years:

You are not guilty, Harriet. At least of this offense.

August 23, 2015
(HARRIET AT SEVENTY-EIGHT)

Harriet is awakened by the squalling of the public address system, signaling the *Zuiderdam*'s imminent arrival in Glacier Bay. Having been up half the night with Caroline, Harriet feels ten years older as she drags herself out of bed to find her daughter on the love seat, flipping absently through *Mariner* magazine.

"Morning, Mom."

"Good morning, dear."

Indeed, it is a good morning. It's overcast, which bodes well. The pamphlets say that the glaciers look their best beneath gray skies.

Upon Caroline's suggestion, they order breakfast from room service, and Wayan soon wheels in their omelets, with a sly wink for Harriet.

"No crab today, eh, Ms. Chance?"

"Good day, Wayan," she says.

The boy smiles. Releasing the cart, he fashions his hands into pincers and snaps them a few times for Harriet's benefit.

"Little smart-ass," she says, upon his departure.

"I don't follow," says Caroline.

"It's a long story. And not one I'm proud of."

They eat side by side on the love seat with the curtains open.

"So, look, I know I've said some crummy things about Dad. But would it be okay if I go with you?"

"Of course, dear. He'd want you there."

Everything feels different after last night. Having cleared the air after all these years, Harriet feels lighter. Her lone regret, aside from the fact that Skip isn't here so she can wring his neck, is that she didn't clear the air thirty years ago.

With Caroline by her side and a chill breeze thundering past her ears, Harriet clutches the yogurt container firmly to her chest. Everything feels wrong for the occasion. It isn't just the indifference of this eternal landscape forged by ice. She failed to consider the crowds, the incessant click of camera shutters, the oohing and aahing, the children darting about, squealing with laughter, horning in on her real estate, and stepping on her toes.

Harriet clutches the ashes still closer as she stares straight ahead into the wind, her eyes fixed on the glacier that is glowing eerily blue against the white backdrop. Beyond its fissured facade, the glacier runs a smooth ribbon of ice into the mountains, through valleys carved violently and patiently over eons as far as the eye can see. Everything about this place—its stillness and scope and magnitude—seems to suggest permanence. But in fifty years, it will be gone.

"Remember those Mentholatum cough drops?" says a voice, startling Harriet from her reverie. "The ones I used to like?"

Harriet turns. There, beside her, in Caroline's place, leaning against the rail in his blue windbreaker, stands Bernard. At ninety, he cuts a stooped figure, hatless, and gaunter than ever. His hair has thinned, now, only a few windblown wisps of white remaining. The hair growing out of his ears, meanwhile, has thickened.

Suddenly the deck all around them is deserted. The children, the camera snappers, have all disappeared without a trace. Caroline is nowhere to be seen. Only Harriet and Bernard remain amid the sprawl of mountain and ice.

"Dirtier than I thought it would be," he observes. "But they really got the color right, didn't they? Halls, I mean."

"Vicks," she says. "Please don't try to talk me out of this, Bernard."

"I wouldn't think of it," he says, looking over his shoulder. "But hurry up. I haven't got much time."

"Why are you here, Bernard? I think you owe me an explanation by now. To warn me, is that it? I want to know why you're happening to me."

"Trust me, I haven't got time to explain. I'd rather just savor these moments."

They trail off into silence, turning their attention overboard, where countless chunks of ice bob on the choppy surface of the bay.

"I forgive you, Bernard."

Bernard fashions a sad smile, gathering a few wisps of hair between his fingers, before smoothing them back.

"You don't have to, you know? That's not why I came. And anyway, I don't deserve it."

"Maybe not," she says. "But forgiveness isn't something you earn."

From the glacier comes a deep rumbling and a yawning, and finally a thunderlike peel, as a massive wedge of ice splinters off the face, splashing down into the bay. Seconds later, the great, still silence returns, impervious to the disruption.

"So it goes," says Bernard, looking over his shoulder. Then without warning, he releases the rail and takes off, trotting lamely down the deck. "Gotta go," he calls. "I'll try to come back."

Harriet watches him struggle with the heavy door to the stairwell, then hobble down two steps before the door closes behind him.

Slowly, she turns back to the rail and fixes her eyes on the massive glacier; for all its ancient grandeur, for all its size and determination, impermanent. And just as sure as the frigid air kisses her face, she feels the cool certainty of death. Though heaven knows she ought to be accustomed to the idea by now, it suddenly occurs to Harriet that she might die sooner rather than later. The yogurt container slips from her grasp. She fumbles to recover it as it crashes to the deck. The lid bursts open. A cloud of soot and ash explode into the wind.

Instinctively, Harriet stoops to gather the remains. But before she can corral the container and the lid, the swarm of ash has dissipated, mingling with the arctic airstream. When she looks up, Harriet finds herself looking at the alarmed countenance of her daughter.

"Mom, Jesus, what's the matter? Are you all right? You're not making any sense."

November 4, 2014
(HARRIET AT SEVENTY-EIGHT)

Happy birthday, Harriet Chance! Consider yourself fortunate to have enjoyed so many. For seventy-eight, you are exceptionally active. Well, maybe not exceptionally, but compared to some, you're a real fireplug. What's on your docket this afternoon, birthday girl? How about breakfast with the St. Luke's fund-raising committee? Did somebody say bake sale? Then it's off to Safeway for some OxiClean and a sponge, where Chad will inform you (for the third time) that his own birthday is June 23 and that he has a cat named Stuart. Also, he will forget to wheel the cart back. Again.

At noon, it's lunch with your pal Mildred at the Crab Pot, where your nearest and dearest friend presents you with an extravagant gift: a Bulova dress diamond-accent wristwatch from Macy's; it must have cost four hundred dollars. You will cherish that watch. For a while. Until you throw it overboard ten months later.

It's too much, you say, really, just too much. But actually, you're thrilled. While the old Timex Bernard gifted you on your silver anniversary is still ticking, it's not much to look at, never was.

Oh, Mildred, it's lovely, you shouldn't have, really.

But what you'd like even more than a wristwatch is for Mildred to accompany you on your afternoon visit to Sherwood Arms. God, but it's so depressing. You're not sure you can do it alone.

But alas, Mildred has a hair appointment. Last time it was the dentist.

When you arrive at Sherwood Arms, and the orderly with the scorpion tattoo escorts you to Bernard's room, you are immediately given reason to hope. While your husband still does not recognize you, he thinks he does. Apparently, he believes you to be the party responsible for stealing his remote control—someone named Simone. The orderly informs you in a gruff whisper that the remote control was not stolen but in fact was confiscated by the night orderly after Bernard was caught gnawing on the device, claiming it was a hoagie.

That he remembers Simone's name is a good sign, right? At least the cheesecloth of his memory is still holding something. They've been working with him. Developing some tools. Helping him manage his limited resources. Yesterday he played an entire game of tic-tac-toe with Dr. Stevens.

He lost, but still, he was in until the end.

Where's my damn remote? he wants to know. What's he doing here? Who is he? Where's Mildred?

Look, Bernard, I've brought you some lemon bars.

Where's my remote?

Yes, all in all, a hopeful visit.

You have this much to be happy about, Harriet: things are moving slower in the wrong direction. And you're okay with that. You feel yourself getting stronger by the day. You can now devote some of your resources to self-care. You've even gone to three support groups in the past two weeks. You're developing a few tools of your own. And of course, your scones were a hit each time.

That's what's so devastating about the call at four in the morning. The female voice on the line is measured, businesslike, as it explains that while wandering the halls, unauthorized and unattended, past midnight, your husband apparently slipped on the travertine floor and hit his head. He was unconscious when Simone found him. More than unconscious, actually.

The fact is, Harriet Chance, your husband is in a coma.

August 23, 2015
(HARRIET AT SEVENTY-EIGHT)

A t lunch, Harriet is . . . what is the word she's looking for, *spacey*? Yes, that's it, *spacey*. My, but it's busy here on the . . . What is this green stuff on my . . . ? What did I do with my, oh, here it is . . .

Her hands, still clutching the empty yogurt container, do not belong to her. Her feet are cinder blocks. Though she's trying to be attentive, her daughter's words are elusive.

"Mom, seriously, I think you might've had a stroke up there, or something. You were saying stuff that didn't make any sense. You tried to grab somebody's camera."

"Did I?"

"You were trying to hold some lady's hand."

"Oh, dear. Darling, what is this green matter on my plate?"

"Chard, I think. Maybe mustard greens. I don't know the difference. Look, Mom, I really think we should see a doctor after lunch, get you checked out. Just to play it safe."

Her hands clutch the yogurt container harder. "Yes, dear. That would be fine," she says, surprised by her own calmness.

"Y'all mind if I join you?" says a morbidly obese fellow, who has materialized suddenly at the end of the table. He's clutching a Caesar salad and wearing a black T-shirt that says I SEE DUMB PEOPLE.

"I owe y'all an apology for last night," he says.

"Last night?" says Harriet.

"I'm the one who owes you an apology," Caroline says. "How were you supposed to know you were dealing with a couple of basket cases?"

"Well now, I wouldn't go that far."

"That's because you're polite," says Caroline.

"Aren't you going to introduce me," says Harriet.

Caroline and the man exchange awkward looks before the man extends a hand. "Kurt Pickens, Owingsville, Kentucky, pleased to meet you, ma'am."

"Harriet Chance," she says.

"So what'd y'all think of them glaciers?"

"Glaciers, dear? Oh yes, glaciers."

"Mom's a little confused this morning," Caroline explains.

"Couldn't barely move with all them people up on deck," Kurt observes. "Thing of it is, I don't know about y'all, but

I felt all alone up there. No matter that the lady behind me kept proddin' me with her camera bag or that some kid nearly upchucked on my shoe. I felt like the last person on earth. Like I was standin' at the pearly gates and everyone else was inside already. Left behind, that's how it felt. Somethin' about all that ice, I reckon. All that big white silence. Put me in the mind to gamble, if you know what I mean?"

"Dear," says Harriet. "Would you happen to know what this green matter on my plate is? It looks like some kind of chard."

That's the last thing Harriet says before she feels the world tilt sideways, as though the ship has been tossed by a giant swell. The next thing she knows, her head is in Mr. Pickens's lap.

Harriet is back to her old self by the time Caroline and Kurt have wheeled her down to the ship's infirmary, where a very tan, bushy-browed, vaguely familiar gentleman named Frankel, wearing a stethoscope, tends to Harriet, though not before he's forced to pry the yogurt container from her grasp.

"Are you diabetic?"

"No," says Harriet.

"Any irregularities in blood sugar?"

"No."

"Low blood pressure?"

"No."

"Hypertension?"

"A little."

"Are you taking any medication?"

"Well, yes, I am taking a number of things."

At length, Harriet lists her prescriptions. Fosamax, Celebrex, and down the line. The doctor begins cocking a brow halfway through the inventory.

"Impressive," he says. "Slowly now, I'm going to ask you to sit up." He cradles her head in his hands as Harriet eases herself upright, Caroline and Wayan lending a hand.

When she's sitting up on the bed, Frankel holds up a finger, instructing Harriet to follow its progress, side to side.

"She's tracking," he announces. "Any nausea?"

"No."

"Palpitations, sweating?"

"No."

"My feet feel heavier than usual, though."

"How long has this been going on? The disorientation?" This query seems to be directed more at Caroline than Harriet.

"Mom?"

"It hasn't," says Harriet.

"So this was just an isolated incident? No history of short term-memory loss?"

"Nothing like this," says Harriet. "It was the strangest thing. One minute, I was—"

"Actually," interjects Caroline. "She's had a couple of episodes recently. Right, Mom?"

Harriet looks down at her lap. "I have been a little out of sorts," she admits.

"She's been having dreams."

"Dreams?"

"About my fa—. About her husband," says Caroline. "He died last year."

"I see. I'm sorry," says Dr. Frankel. "First, I'm going to recommend rest. This could simply be a little hypoperfusion we're dealing with, exacerbated by exhaustion, shock, any number of things." Or," he says, "there could be another pathology at work. You don't remember anything from this morning?"

"Nothing before the buffet."

"And last night?"

"Not much."

"Okay, here's what I recommend," Frankel says, more to Caroline than Harriet. "That you take it easy in Ketchikan. In fact, I'm going to have to insist. Not trying to scare you here, but I don't want to rule out the possibility of something more serious. When you return to the states, you undergo some testing. I'd schedule a CT right away. Rule out a few possibilities. Find out what—if anything—is going on here. No reason to speculate and no reason to panic. I'm not ready to call this anything. This is nothing too out of the ordinary for someone her age. But . . ."

Harriet doesn't like the way he said but. Or the way he left it hanging there. Like he knew something. She tries to chase away a sudden uneasiness.

"Will it happen again?" says Caroline.

"There's really no way of knowing. It could, yes. Which is why I insist you take it easy. And I think it's best that some-body stay with her at all times. We wouldn't want her taking a fall. If there's any pressure building in there, we wouldn't want . . . look, just take it easy. Schedule the tests."

As Caroline and Kurt wheel her back to the cabin, Harriet finds herself embarrassed by all the fuss. For once, she wishes she were invisible.

"This wheelchair is totally unnecessary," she complains, still clutching the empty yogurt tub.

"Mom, you heard him, you're supposed to take it easy."

"Y'all are welcome to push me instead," says Kurt breathlessly.

"Really, Mom. Don't be stubborn. I know this is tough for you. But you just gotta go with the program."

More than frightened, more than humbled, even, Harriet is grateful for Caroline's presence. She seems so much more to-gether, so much more capable than she was forty-eight hours ago.

At the cabin door, Harriet and Caroline thank Kurt and bid him farewell.

"He's nice," says Caroline after she shuts the door.

In spite of Harriet's protestations, Caroline clutches her under the arms, assisting her out of the wheelchair and onto the bed, then promptly turns on the television without asking.

"Do you want any water or anything, Mom?"

"No, dear, thank you."

"Are you hungry?"

"Not in the least."

"Look, just stay put for a few minutes, okay? I've gotta go down the hall for a sec."

"Where are you going?"

"I've gotta let Skip know what's going on."

"Frankly, I don't see as how he's entitled to an update, Caroline. For heaven's sake, he tried to swindle his own mother. All he ever had to do is ask. He didn't even have the courage to do it himself. Let him sweat it out, Caroline. Let him think about his actions."

"Mom, I told him I'd let him know. He really does worry about you, that much is true."

On her way out the door, Caroline indicates the empty yogurt container with a nod.

"And Mom," she says. "Maybe it's time to let go, huh?"

November 8, 2014
(HARRIET AT SEVENTY-EIGHT)

As far as decisions go, you've certainly made worse in your day, possibly even more far-reaching, considering your husband is ninety years old, and let's face it, nobody's been busy planning a birthday party. But you've never made a decision quite this difficult. Yes, on one level it's a no-brainer (sorry, bad metaphor), but on another level it's unthinkable (oops, did it again).

If that first drive to Sherwood Arms was long, the drive to St. Joseph Med in Tacoma is interminable. Once again, you slump in the backseat of Skip's SUV, which smells even more florid than usual. This you know, because Skip keeps politely cracking his window.

None of this seems real. It feels as if somebody, without warning, has pulled the plug on the rest of your life.

Okay, bad metaphor again.

The point is, more than anything else, the suddenness of your grief has you reeling. You have no idea what your life looks like after today. Hard as you try, you can't even see tomorrow.

You hate seeing him this way, arranged corpselike, lips and extremities bloodless, respirators jammed up his nose, heart monitors beating, IVs dripping. This is even less your Bernard than was the man who recently spit in your face and accused you of trying to poison him, the man who tried to eat a remote control. But none of this makes it any easier, does it, Harriet? Because some part of you wants to believe there's still hope. You've got to believe. You weren't sleeping all those years in church.

Maybe the fall jarred something, you tell yourself. Maybe he'll snap out of this coma and miraculously remember everything, and the two of you can go back to your contentious Scrabble matches, your early dinners, and the stultifying routine that marked your days before Bernard began losing his mind.

Even if he didn't remember you, that wouldn't be so bad.

Even if he returned to Sherwood Arms, and you made your daily visits and baked him lemon ginger scones, that would be okay. Even if he just lay here like this, insensate, maybe twitching an eyebrow now and again, wiggling a toe, as you read the history of the Civil War to him or combed his hair and trimmed his fingernails, that wouldn't be the worst thing in the world.

No, this is the worst thing in the world: reality. Trumper of hope, killer of faith. The reality that there's no going back, that once those monitors stop beeping, the only man you've ever loved will never again hold your hand or touch your shoulder or berate you for a dripping faucet.

When Skip and Caroline leave the room, you stand there stupidly, all alone in the chill hospital air, not knowing what to do or say as the life support ceases functioning.

"I'm sorry it ended badly," you say.

He's already dead, you tell yourself. There is little significance to this moment. But something happens, doesn't it, Harriet? As you watch his chest rise and fall for the last time, watch his ribs contract with the tiniest of paroxysms, you actually feel him take leave, not of his own body but of yours, like a shiver running from the base of your neck out the top of your head.

Only then do you realize that all these years he lived inside of you.

August 24, 2015
(HARRIET AT SEVENTY-EIGHT)

Caroline's been gone less than two minutes when Harriet feels a familiar presence beside her in bed: Bernard.

"I've been thinking," he says from behind the cover of his newspaper. "Maybe cut Skipper a little slack," he says. "He's desperate, you know."

"That's what Caroline says."

"She'd know."

"But selling my house from under me, locking me away in a nursing home? And not even having the courage to do it himself. What really gets me is he could have just asked for help."

Bernard lowers his newspaper, his eyes scanning the room

nervously. "We all could have. The point is, Skip's on the ropes. Hell, half of America is. He's not in his right mind, at least he wasn't when he hatched this ridiculous plot. It's amazing the things we can talk ourselves into when we're desperate for a result. And really, maybe it's not such a bad plan, after all. You're gonna break your neck on those basement stairs one of these days if you're not careful. You can't possibly handle that big yard by yourself."

"I chose that house. And I choose it still."

"Whatever you say. I'm running out of time here. We both are, Harriet. You forgave Caroline. Now forgive Skip. Go easy on him."

"I went pretty easy on you, didn't I?"

"You did, yes. And forgive yourself while you're at it. That's the biggest one of all."

They retreat into silence. After a moment, Bernard peels the covers back, rolls up his newspaper like a baton, taps it decisively once upon his lap, and climbs out of bed.

"Well, I think this is it, Harriet."

"You're leaving?"

"I have to. No time to explain, but I haven't got a choice."

"What will happen to me?"

"I can't tell you that."

"Can't or won't?"

Standing now, he looks down on her sympathetically. "Amounts to the same thing. I'm sorry I made a mess of us. Of everything, really. I could have been more, a lot more."

"What will happen to you?"

"Nothing."

God, but Harriet wants to reach out and touch him one last time, to grab hold of him and never let go. But she's stuck in place, unable to budge, held there in bed by some invisible force akin to gravity.

"What are you?" she says. "You owe me that much. A ghost, an angel, a dream?"

Crow's-feet bunch at the corners of his eyes. "It's not for me to say."

There's something timeless etched beneath their gray-green veneer, some truth or recognition regarding the nature of existence, some celestial reckoning, Harriet is sure of it. But hard as she tries to apprehend it, it is simply beyond her reach.

Bernard backs away from the bed slowly, a sheepish smile on his face. "Well, here goes nothing," he says.

In that instant, the key latch clicks and the cabin door swings open.

Still backing away, Bernard blows her a kiss.

"Don't go," she says.

"Mom?" says Caroline, from the doorway. "What's up? You're doing it again."

"No, no, dear. Just thinking aloud."

When Harriet turns back to Bernard, he's gone, disappeared into thin air.

Caroline stoops to pick Bernard's rolled-up newspaper off

of the floor, tossing it absently on the coffee table. "Maybe Ketchikan is too much, Mom. Maybe we should just stay aboard tomorrow, watch some movies, order room service."

"Heavens, no," says Harriet. "I wouldn't hear of it. It's our last stop, dear."

July 4, 1938
(HARRIET AT ONE)

My, but how we've grown, Harriet! To think, from a scrawny six pounds and change, we're now officially off the charts at twenty months. Our neck disappeared at three months. Our arms and legs ballooned. When we smile, we have more chins than teeth.

Everybody expected us to start thinning out after our first birthday, once we started walking. But we still look as though we've got rubber bands around our wrists and ankles. Our mother calls us "Little Piggy" even as she foists another formula bottle full of powdered milk and Karo syrup on us. She may as well be injecting it into our thighs. We yearn for real food, but for reasons we will never understand, our mother forever pushes the bottle on us.

Our father adores us, every ounce. Not without pride, he characterizes us as his "little bruiser."

Ample. Substantial. Tubby. All words used to describe our one-and-a-half-year-old personage. Quiet, of course, is another.

No, we've still yet to utter a sound, Harriet, beyond the occasional yelp, sniffle, or burp. What are we waiting for? Nobody's expecting sentences, Little Piggy. A few grunts would suffice, even some crying would be a welcome development. While nobody can fault us for our stoicism, they'd like to know that we're at least capable of utterance.

Speak, Harriet, it's in your best interest!

A simple "Help!" might have come in handy on that fateful Fourth of July 1938 as friends and family of Nathan, Montgomery, Ferris, and Fitzsimmons gather to celebrate American independence.

Look at us, Harriet, squatting beneath a picnic table at Volunteer Park, staring at our mother's swollen ankles, inhaling the blue smoke of the barbecue, and listening to the muffled laughter of other children as a greedy bite of frankfurter, scavenged from beneath the table, lodges itself in our esophagus.

Silently, we panic as our eyes bulge from their sockets.

Quietly we gasp for dear life as the inky black ghosts crowd our vision. This is it, Harriet. Say something! Speak, child!

Okay, the truth is, we couldn't have made a sound if we wanted to, not with that hot dog wedged in our gullet.

Consider us lucky, Harriet.

Our frantic kicks alert the second-nearest adult, who finding us bug-eyed and blue at his feet, pulls us out, and promptly executes his version of the Heimlich maneuver. In dislodging the offending sausage, he inadvertently breaks two of our ribs, a fact that will not be discovered until late the following afternoon when the bruising becomes impossible to ignore.

Still, he saved our life, Charlie Fitzsimmons. Not that we owe him anything. I mean, it's only one life.

But let's not dwell on debts, Harriet. Instead, let's talk about the moment, that instant when we leave our body, when we feel our mother's legs, the grass, and the whole world begin to recede, as though down a dark vortex. Let's talk about that millisecond of instinct, that invisible force that seizes us, body and soul, and pulls us back into the world, just as sure as Uncle Charlie drags us out from under the table by the ankles.

That invisible force, that was you, Harriet, that was us, before we parted ways, wanting to live.

August 25, 2015
(HARRIET AT SEVENTY-EIGHT)

It's sixty degrees and drizzling when Harriet, Caroline, and Kurt disembark in the bustling port of Ketchikan, the cruise's final scheduled stop. According to the pamphlets, this rain-battered hamlet of eight thousand is Alaska's southeasternmost city and also its most densely populated. A working-class town smelling of barnacles and rust, wood rot, and diesel smoke, wet dog hair in heaters, and fish nets hung out to dry. Despite civic-minded efforts to splash some vibrant color about, there's no disguising the town's blimp gray underbelly.

Kurt guides Harriet's wheelchair down along the piers, among the kiosks and buses and herds of grazing tourists. She's found an unlikely new companion in Kurt Pickens. On the bus ride to the Saxman Native Village, he sits directly across the aisle from her, taking up two seats. Once again, he's clean-shaven, and wearing a T-shirt (with sleeves, Harriet notes with satisfaction), announcing I'M A VIRGIN (BUT THIS IS AN OLD SHIRT).

"Y'all are sure you don't mind me tagging along now?"

"Why, dear, we invited you, didn't we?" says Harriet.

The bus is an ancient charter with blistered paint, squeaky seats, and a clattering diesel engine. The tour guide, whom Harriet can barely hear over the din of the engine, though spirited and delightfully informative, has an unfortunately lazy *s*: "To the thouth, you'll thee Printh Rupert Thound."

Pressing her face to the window, Harriet gazes out as the creaky old charter hugs the fog-tattered narrows along a two-lane highway. She learns all about Ketchikan and Revilla-gigedo Islands, learns of the 150 inches of rain per year, the world-renown fishing, the defunct brothels and pulp mills, along with its protected forests and misty fiords. She learns about the Tlingit people, a matrilineal culture of clans, the People of the Tides, as they call themselves.

At the Saxman Village, the bus empties into a mist of rain, its cargo spreading out toward the Clan House and the gift shop and the grand totem poles, arranged in lines and half circles throughout the village. Kurt and Caroline take turns pushing Harriet from one pole to the next, where Kurt reads the placards aloud.

"How 'bout that? Says here inanimate objects were forbidden on totems—only living things could be portrayed. Seems to me, I seen one out near Pikeville with a hamburger on it, but I reckon it wasn't Tlingit."

The carvings are at turns playful and menacing, mischievous and somber. Harriet is particularly compelled by the stories they tell. The clan histories: Eagle and Raven and on down the line to Bear and Frog and Fox, Wolf and Beaver. The narratives of a people and the histories they cannot outrun. The inheritance of identity, committed to form, displayed for all the world to acknowledge. All the humiliations, tragedies, quarrels, debts, and shames bequeathed them through the unyielding cycle of generations. And other tellings, anecdotal by comparison: a birth, a wedding, a funeral. And on the edge of the village, away from the rest of the totems, a lone pole, faded and weather-beaten, telling the story of a child's mysterious disappearance. For the second time in two days, Harriet intimates her impending death.

"What's wrong, Mom?" says Caroline when she sees that Harriet's eyes are misting over.

"It's nothing, dear."

Kurt clears his throat. "Well, think I'll mosey on over to the gift shop."

Harriet and Caroline watch him lumber off down the gravel path, Harriet wiping her eyes. Halfway there, Kurt turns and points up at the sky.

"Y'all see that?" he shouts.

A pair of bald eagles, maybe two hundred yards off, bank

high and wide in the southern sky. Harriet and Caroline watch them arc to the east, then circle north into the wind until they glide westward, not fifty yards above the Clan House.

"They make it look easy," says Harriet.

In the gift shop, Caroline parks her directly in front of an end-cap display of miniature totem poles, then drifts toward the racks of postcards. Kurt is in the far corner, thumbing through Native art. When no one is looking, pride insists that Harriet abandon her wheelchair and hobble outside, around the corner to the portable bathroom, which she's relieved to find well maintained.

Afterward, she pulls her pants up and straightens her hair in the blurry mirror. When she makes to leave, she finds the doorknob uncooperative. Inadvertently, she has managed to lock herself in the bathroom. Fiddling with the lock, she finds that the mechanism won't budge. She knocks and knocks on the door, but nobody seems to hear her. She twists the knob, finesses it, jiggles it every which way, without success.

"Hello?" she says. "Is anybody out there?"

Outside, in the distance, she hears the throaty rattle of the bus's diesel engine as it fires up. She pounds the door a little harder, with a hollow thunk-thunk-thunk.

"Hello, hello," she says. "In here! Can somebody help me?"

Relax, she tells herself. Somebody's bound to need the bathroom before long. They couldn't possibly leave without her. Caroline wouldn't allow it. They're probably looking for her right this minute. Still, she continues twisting the knob this way and that, kicking the door with her tiny orthopedic shoe, until after five minutes she's arrived at a considerable state of anxiety. God, don't let it be here. Not in a public restroom!

"Help! Somebody! In here!"

Suddenly she feels a pinch at the back of her skull, and just like that, she's got a headache.

"Somebody, please," she says. "In here!"

Her limbs go heavy in an instant as her vision begins to blur. Dizzy, she lowers herself back down on the toilet, her heart beating rapidly.

"Somebody help me," she says breathlessly as her anxiety edges toward panic. Stay calm, she tells herself, it's only a spell. She quiets her breathing enough to call out again. "In here!"

Just as her heart starts picking up speed again, the doorknob begins to jiggle from the outside, then two brisk knocks.

"Y'all in there, Harriet? The bus is fixin' to leave."

Oh, thank God for Kurt Pickens, her knight in shining armor!

"Dear, I'm locked in. The doorknob is broken."

"Well now, just hold tight. I'll be right back."

She hears his heavy footsteps down the gravel path.

Within minutes, Kurt returns with the proprietor, who, at some length, begins liberating Harriet with the aid of an electric drill and what sounds like a sizable mallet. With her impending release, Harriet's anxiety abates. Her dizziness subsides. Her heart slows, and her breathing returns to normal, though her slight headache persists, little more than a pinprick of pressure at the base of her skull. Nothing half a Vicodin can't fix.

Outside, the weather is breaking.

"Thank God, you heard me," says Harriet, clutching his huge hand.

"Y'all don't honestly think we'd forget you?"

As Harriet resumes her seat on the bus, the sun is fighting its way through the clouds. Whatever happened back there in the bathroom has passed. Harriet feels her strength returning with each breath. Her thoughts regain their sharpness. All things considered, she's cautiously optimistic that she's not dying.

On the edge of town, the bus squawks to an abrupt halt alongside a guano-streaked retaining wall, triggering an explosion of seagulls. One gull remains on the concrete perch after the others have scattered. A miserable creature from all appearances, disheveled and stained, hopping listlessly along on one leg, the other leg missing completely. There's clearly a problem with the remaining leg. As the bird hops closer, Harriet sees that above the lone foot a wire bread tie is wound hopelessly around its ankle, so snug it almost looks as if the leg has started to grow around it. The best it can do is drag the wire along behind it. Eventually, the handicap will catch up with it, Harriet figures, and the bird will be unable to care for itself, and it will die. Until then, it will suffer, with no better sense than to try and survive.

After a few hops along the wall, it arrives directly in front of Harriet's window, not two feet from her face, where it stops and looks in on her intently, as though it thinks she might have something for it. She wishes she did—it surprises her how much she wishes. As the bus pulls away with a groan and a black belch of diesel, Harriet feels, for the second time in an hour, her eyes begins to mist over.

But for a slight headache, Harriet is back to normal by the time the bus drops them downtown. Caroline pilots the wheelchair along the wharf, past the kiosks and gem shops, then up the hill and back down, Kurt wheezing like a ruptured balloon. The three of them converse pleasantly on a host of subjects.

In the afternoon, they eat lunch right on the water, the surf lapping at the piles beneath their feet, the gulls sounding their urgent cries. Harriet orders salmon cooked on a cedar plank, garnished with lemon and dill. Kurt orders a chopped salad, and when that's not enough to curb his appetite, he refills his water three times and bravely gnaws on an orange rind. Caroline seems perfectly at ease sipping her club soda, now and then turning her face to the wind. The monkey's fist never leaves her purse.

It's not every day that there's order in the universe, Harriet Chance, so enjoy this: Breathe deeply of that salty air, really let it fill your lungs. Feel that coho melt on your tongue, feel it slide down your throat like butter. Sink into that easy conversation. Feel that breeze blowing through your thin, white hair. Taste that lemon, Harriet. Wince with pain and pleasure. Laugh, sigh, and massage your aching joints under the table. And while you're at it, take a good long look at your smiling daughter across the table, the lines of her face moving in new directions, one hour, one day at a time. Recognize and give thanks for the crisp edges and heightened sensations of these moments, for they are precious. Remember them until you are no longer able.

Live, Harriet, live! Live like this salty breath is your last.

August 26, 2015
(HARRIET AT SEVENTY-EIGHT)

Back on the *Zuiderdam*, Harriet boards the elevator with Caroline and Kurt. Other than the slight headache, she can't complain, although it's true that she's suddenly very tired. And something else, slightly giddy, and now that you mention it, a little lightheaded. And then there's the slight pinching at the base of her skull, which is not part of the general headache, but something sharper.

"Y'all were swell, having me along for the day," says Kurt. "Those eagles were somethin' else. How about you, Harriet, what was your favorite part?"

When Harriet doesn't answer, Caroline intercedes, seizing her elbow gently.

"Mom."

"Yes, dear?"

"Kurt just asked you a question."

"Oh. What was it, dear?"

"What was the highlight for you? Today, I mean."

Somehow Harriet is staring at her own reflection, and this is confusing.

"I think I liked the eagles," Kurt rejoins, after a pause.

"Mom," says Caroline, squeezing her elbow harder. "What was the highlight?"

The question, like the reflection staring back at her, is disorienting. Even as the elevator begins to rise, Harriet has forgotten where she is.

"You okay, Mom?"

"Oh. Yes."

The truth is, Harriet is woozy—very woozy, in fact. All her blood seems to be rushing to her legs.

"Mom, you don't look good."

When the elevator door opens, Caroline leads Harriet out by the elbow. Harriet can hardly keep her eyes open as she steps onto the hideous carpet of Rotterdam.

"I think we should get a doctor," she hears Caroline say.

Then Harriet is weightless.

When she open her eyes, Caroline and Kurt are as two disembodied heads floating above her. Their mouths are moving, and though Harriet can hear the dull intonations of their voice, just above the rushing of blood in her ears, she has no idea what they're saying.

August 26, 2015
(HARRIET AT SEVENTY-EIGHT)

You've been fading in and out the past hour or so. Strangely, you're in less pain than usual. Apparently, among your body's diminished capacities is the capacity to feel discomfort. Mostly, you feel feverish and slow-witted, as they wheel you down the corridor in a gurney and up the elevator to the open air of the observation deck.

The wind stirs the downy hairs on your face, as you clutch your daughter's hand.

"It's gonna be okay, Mom."

You are calm, almost complacent, as your thoughts slow to a trickle and the blood runs thick through your veins. Soon you hear a distant thrumming, like rolling thunder from beyond the hills. The sound draws progressively nearer, until it's deafening, and your white hair is blowing crazily, and your teeth are practically chattering from the vibration.

Caroline sits with you in the medivac, still clutching your hand. Gently encouraging you to relax, not to worry. You want to tell her that you love her, but you can't. You should have told her a long time ago, but now you can hardly move your lips. Your voice is a wisp, unintelligible over the thundering blades of the chopper.

Above you, the clouds are breaking. You manage to raise your head a few inches and tilt it just slightly. Look once more at the world, three hundred feet below, the silver expanse of choppy ocean, like hammered steel, the furrowed green foothills to the east, and the great sudden mountains crouching patiently beyond. At five hundred feet, you can see the curvature of the earth. Fear not, Harriet, it will keep spinning in your absence.

If we've learned one thing digging up all these old bones, dusting them off, and holding them to the light, we've learned this: While the days unfold, one after the other, and the numbers all move in one direction, our lives are not linear, Harriet. We are the sum of moments and reflections, actions and decisions, triumphs, failures, and yearnings, all of it held together, inexplicably, miraculously, really, by memory and association. Yes, Harriet, our lives are more sinew than bone.

As the sun, in its waning, westerly aspect, slants pinkly through the chopper window, you feel, for the first time since you were a toddler, the irrepressible pull of that vortex toward some distant horizon.

Acknowledgments

The author would like to gratefully acknowledge to following people: first, the courageous women in my life, the women who have nurtured me, educated me, disciplined me, sacrificed for me, suffered for me, and never forsaken me; my mom, my grandma, my sisters, my wife, and my third grade teacher, Mrs. Hanford, to name a few. The women who have often settled for less, the women who've never quite gotten their fair share, who have soldiered on in the face of inequity, frustration, and despair, who have forgiven beyond reasonable measure, absorbed beyond reasonable expectation, and given, given, given with no promise of recompense. I wanted to thank them with this portrait of one woman, inspired by all of them, from the moment of her conception, to her last breath.

Also, for their input, collaboration, and support: Mollie Glick, Emily Brown, Chuck "Pops" Adams, Kelly Bowen, Craig Popelars, Lauren Moseley, Brunson Hoole, Jude Grant, Brooke Csuka, Elisabeth Scharlatt, Debra Linn, and everyone else at the Gonk. For their inspiration and assistance: Rebecca and Tim Dowling, Bryan Roper, Lydia Williams, Jessie Jameson, Janet Woodman, and MaryJo Caruso. And finally, a big thanks to my early readers: Mark Krieger, Joseph Rakowski, Joshua Mohr, and Aaron Cance.